London Borough of Hounslow

Library Services

...uld be retu... ...latest date
...not re... ...you may
...on o... ...only). Please
...y car... ...charge will be made for
...rene...ed after th...

MISSION SURVIVAL

LAIR OF THE LEOPARD

www.**randomhousechildrens**.co.uk

C0000 002 741 969

CHARACTER PROFILES

Beck Granger

At just fourteen years old, Beck Granger knows more about the art of survival than most military experts learn in a lifetime. When he was young he travelled with his parents to some of the most remote places in the world, from Antarctica to the African Bush, and he picked up many vital survival skills from the remote tribes he met along the way.

Uncle Al

Professor Sir Alan Granger is one of the world's most respected anthropologists. His stint as a judge on a reality television show made him a household name, but to Beck he will always be plain old Uncle Al – more comfortable in his lab with a microscope than hob-nobbing with the rich and famous. He believes that patience is a virtue and has a 'never-say-die' attitude to life. For the past few years he has been acting as guardian to Beck, who has come to think of him as a second father.

David & Melanie Granger

Beck's mum and dad were Special Operations Directors for the environmental direct action group, Green Force. Together with Beck, they spent time with remote tribes in some of the world's most extreme places. Several years ago their light plane mysteriously crashed in the jungle. Their bodies were never found and the cause of the accident remains unexplained . . .

James Blake

James is tall and broad-shouldered, and a year older than Beck. His mother, Abby Blake, wanted him to go into the family business but James decided, after much soul searching, that it wasn't right for him. Now he's one of the only allies Beck Granger has in the world . . .

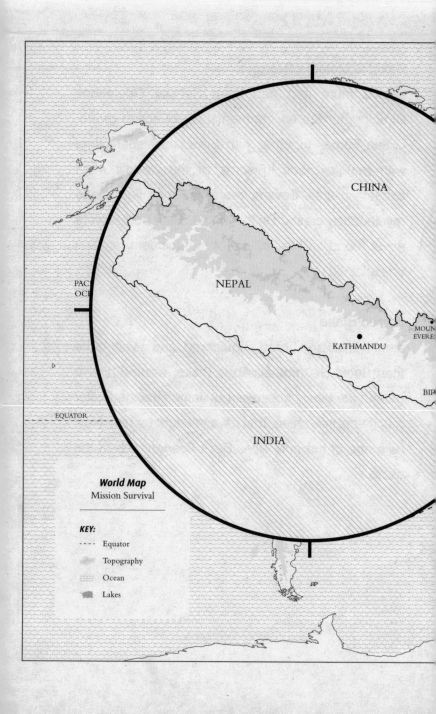

CHINA

PAC
OCE

NEPAL

KATHMANDU

MOUN
EVERE

BIR

EQUATOR

INDIA

World Map
Mission Survival

KEY:
---- Equator
Topography
Ocean
Lakes

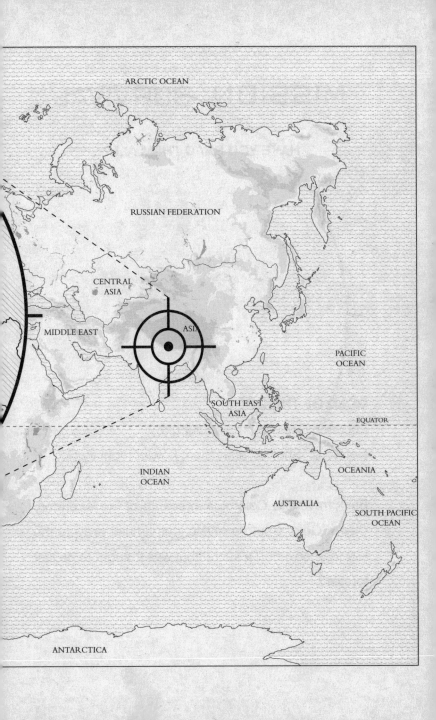

MISSIONSURVIVAL

HAVE YOU READ THEM ALL?

GOLD OF THE GODS

Location: The Colombian Jungle

Dangers: Snakes; starvation; howler monkeys

Beck travels to Colombia in search of the legendary City of Gold. Could a mysterious amulet provide the key to uncovering a secret that was thought to be lost forever?

WAY OF THE WOLF

Location: The Alaskan Mountains

Dangers: Snow storms; wolves; white-water rapids

After his plane crashes in the Alaskan wilderness, Beck has to stave off hunger and the cold as he treks through the frozen mountains in search of help.

SANDS OF THE SCORPION

Location: The Sahara Desert

Dangers: Diamond smugglers; heatstroke; scorpions

Beck is forced into the Sahara Desert to escape a gang of diamond smugglers. Can he survive the heat and evade the smugglers as he makes his way back to safety?

TRACKS OF THE TIGER

Location: The Indonesian Wilderness

Dangers: Volcanoes; tigers; orang-utans

When a volcanic eruption strands him in the jungles of Indonesia, Beck must test his survival skills against red-hot lava, a gang of illegal loggers, and the tigers that are on his trail . . .

CLAWS OF THE CROCODILE

Location: The Australian Outback

Dangers: Flash floods; salt-water crocodiles; deadly radiation

Beck heads to the Outback in search of the truth about the plane crash that killed his parents. But somebody wants the secret to remain hidden – and they will kill to protect it.

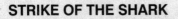

STRIKE OF THE SHARK

Location: The Bermuda Triangle

Dangers: Tiger sharks; hurricanes; dehydration

When Beck Granger is shipwrecked in the open seas, he needs all his survival skills to save a small group of passengers. But the sinking was no accident. In order to stay alive, he'll have to work out who wants him dead. That is, if the sharks don't get him first . . .

RAGE OF THE RHINO

Location: South African savannah

Dangers: Rhino poachers; deadly fires; African wild dogs

Beck Granger is on a mission to stop the poachers targeting rhinos in South Africa. But he soon discovers that he has fallen into a dangerous trap. He has enemies who will stop at nothing to track him down.

LAIR OF THE LEOPARD

A RED FOX BOOK 978 1 849 41838 6

First published in Great Britain by Red Fox
an imprint of Random House Children's Publishers UK
A Penguin Random House Group Company

Penguin
Random House
UK

This edition published 2015

1 3 5 7 9 10 8 6 4 2

Copyright © Bear Grylls, 2015
Cover artwork © Paul Carpenter, 2015
Map artwork © Ben Hasler, 2015

The right of Bear Grylls to be identified as the author of this work has been asserted
in accordance with the Copyright, Designs and Patents Act 1988.

All rights reserved. No part of this publication may be reproduced, stored in a
retrieval system, or transmitted in any form or by any means, electronic, mechanical,
photocopying, recording or otherwise, without the prior permission of the publishers.

Penguin Random House is committed to a sustainable future for our business,
our readers and our planet. This book is made from Forest Stewardship Council®
certified paper.

Set in 11/19 pt Swiss 721 BT by Falcon Oast Graphic Art Ltd.

RANDOM HOUSE CHILDREN'S PUBLISHERS UK
61–63 Uxbridge Road, London W5 5SA

www.randomhousechildrens.co.uk
www.randomhouse.co.uk

Addresses for companies within The Random House Group Limited can be found at:
www.randomhouse.co.uk/offices.htm

THE RANDOM HOUSE GROUP Limited Reg. No. 954009

A CIP catalogue record for this book is available from the British Library.

Printed and bound by CPI Group (UK) Ltd, Croydon, CR0 4YY

MISSION SURVIVAL
LAIR OF THE
LEOPARD

BEAR GRYLLS

RED FOX

BEAR GRYLLS is one of the world's most famous adventurers. After spending three years in the SAS he set off to explore the globe in search of even bigger challenges. He has climbed Mount Everest, crossed the Sahara Desert and circumnavigated Britain on a jet-ski. His TV shows have been seen by more than 1.2 billion viewers in more than 150 countries. In 2009, Bear became Chief Scout to the Scouting Association. He lives in London and Wales with his wife Shara and their three sons: Jesse, Marmaduke and Huckleberry.

To my special nieces and nephews: Mungo,
Bevan, Tallulah, Benjie, Hamish and Saskia.
Adventurous, kind and fun.

Prologue
PART I

'It's like I always say,' said Melanie Granger. The gentle roar of the jet's engines filled the small cabin. It was a compact executive business jet and she and her husband David were the only two passengers. 'We move like the leopard, silently stalking its prey, and they won't even know we're about to take them down until it's too late.'

David had closed his eyes the moment he slumped down in his seat. He opened them again and glanced at his wife.

'Leopards.' He managed a small, brave smile. He never liked to let her see when he was worried, or afraid, or uncertain. Or, in this particular case, all three. 'Of course.'

That was how they had met. They had come together on a conservation course when they were both junior members of Green Force, the environmental action group. Leopards had been Melanie's special project.

They had joined Green Force because they wanted to save the world. Neither of them could have known it would come to this: racing through the skies with evidence that could bring down the Earth's deadliest enemy.

In Melanie's pocket was a hard drive. On that hard drive was every single fact and dirty little truth they could find about a particular company – documents, videos, sound files, spreadsheets. Once that hard drive was with the authorities, the company would be blown wide open and the world would be a better place.

David had been the one to fly them this far. Now he had finally been persuaded to hand over to the co-pilot and get some rest. He didn't want to use the autopilot – autopilots can be reprogrammed. The people they were up against could certainly have managed a little thing like that. They could have taken the plane over and crashed it into the sea. So David had flown them from Australia to Singapore to refuel, and then onwards for the final leg of the journey to Bangkok.

The co-pilot had finally insisted that he take a break, and so he had come back to join his wife in the cabin. The co-pilot was a woman provided by the company they had hired the plane from. David hadn't wanted a co-pilot for the same reason he didn't want to use an autopilot – you don't know you can trust them – but international airline regulations insisted that the plane had two pilots.

Melanie's hand found his and gave it a squeeze. 'We've got everything.' She patted her pocket. 'Everything. This will take Lumos down for good.' She paused. 'Al's expecting us?'

'Spoke to him on the radio thirty minutes ago. He'll be there.'

Alan Granger, David's brother, was waiting in Bangkok to receive the evidence they had collected. He didn't yet know what this was all about but he was in for one heck of a surprise. David and Melanie would then return to Australia and pick up their boy,

Beck, from the capable hands they had left him in. They would have been gone less than twelve hours. No one would have even missed them.

'I wonder if we should have told Beck,' Melanie murmured.

David shook his head. 'Couldn't risk this getting out. You know what we're up against, Mel. These people will stop at nothing to keep this evidence from going public. And I mean, *nothing*. Absolutely—'

'Nothing,' said a woman's voice, over the click of a gun.

Melanie hadn't seen the co-pilot come out of the cockpit. She was a slender woman with short blonde hair. She could have been beautiful, with a face that smiled at you from advertisements. But the eyes were dark and cold, and showed no mercy.

'You've got so many things wrong, Mr Granger,' she said. 'But you got that right, at least. How sad you didn't take the hint. You could have stayed at home and minded your own business, and then none of us would have to be here now.'

'Who the heck are you?' David asked.

'Just call me Abby.'

Abby, Melanie thought at once. *Short for Abigail.* And then her blood ran cold as she worked it out. 'Abigail Blake.'

The gun swung towards her and the other woman smiled. 'Very good, Mrs Granger.'

David had gone pale. 'Blake,' he said, 'as in . . .'

'As in Edwin Blake, my father, the head of Lumos. The man you are trying to destroy. He can't allow that to happen, Mr Granger. And neither can I. He badly wants to see you two, so that is where we're going.'

Melanie's thoughts spun furiously as she stared at the gun. She was under no illusions about trying to outrun a bullet. It didn't work. Abby could have shot them both before they even spotted her.

However, Melanie could not help noticing that she hadn't done it yet. What did this woman intend?

'So, what happens now?' she asked. She took great care to keep her voice unthreatening, though her mouth was dry.

Abby's smile tightened. 'First, you give me the item in your pocket.'

Melanie and David exchanged wide-eyed glances.

All their hard work – pulling the evidence together in the first place, hiding it, making their plans – and this woman knew about it anyway!

Melanie reached into her coat and slowly drew out a compact portable hard drive.

'Throw it onto that seat, there.'

Abby used the gun to point across the cabin. Melanie chucked it gently over so that it landed on the cushion. It was a safe distance away now. Abby could pick it up and slide it into her own pocket without any danger of them jumping her.

'It's backed up, you know,' David said.

Abby laughed merrily. 'Of course it is. On a second hard drive, which is in a bank vault in Sydney. Which has just been destroyed in what the authorities will say is a gas explosion.'

Melanie stared at the square lump in Abby's coat pocket and felt sick at heart. That was all their evidence! Years of preparation! That little hard drive was the most precious thing— No, she corrected herself, the second most precious thing to her in the whole world.

'And now what?' she asked.

'We sit and wait.'

'They're expecting us in Bangkok,' David pointed out. 'There'll be an alert if we don't turn up.'

'I've already filed an alternative flight plan. Bangkok is no longer expecting us. You were very wise not to let your brother in on this, Mr Granger. Otherwise I would have had to go after him too.'

'Alternative flight plan?' David asked. 'Where to?'

Melanie glanced out of the window. The sun had shifted round. The change in course had been so gradual that they hadn't noticed it. 'We're heading north-west,' she said. What lay in that direction? Names of countries ran through her head. Burma. Bangladesh. India. Nepal. China . . . After that, the plane would surely run out of fuel. So, which was it?

Abby sat down in one of the rear-facing seats. The muzzle of the gun didn't waver.

'You'll find out,' she said, with a smile that froze the air.

Prologue
PART II

After that, there was nothing to do but sit and look at the gun. The autopilot did its job and flew them towards their unknown destination. Melanie marvelled at Abby's self-control. She almost didn't seem human. She didn't grow tired. Her arm apparently never ached with holding a heavy weapon. She kept it pointed at them and that was all there was to it.

Once or twice David tried to talk to her. Melanie recognized what he was doing. They had both had hostage training. Field workers for Green Force might expect to be held captive in the course of their work. They were trained to form a bond with their captors. If their captors saw them as fellow humans, then they might be treated better.

It might have worked with someone else, but it had no effect on Abby Blake. Perhaps she had had the same training. Or maybe she just didn't regard other humans as important. Eventually David gave up.

It had grown dark outside the windows when a beeping sound interrupted Melanie's thoughts. Abby seemed to come back to life. She glanced at the autopilot screen in the cockpit.

'Five minutes,' she said. She unbuckled her seat-belt and stood. 'Excellent. Dead on time. So to speak. Soon be there.'

David frowned and glanced out of the window. 'If we land in five minutes, we should have started our descent by now.'

'Who said anything about landing? This is where I'm getting off.' Abby headed towards the end of the cabin.

'But . . .' Melanie blurted. 'You said your father wanted to see us!'

'True, I did, yes. I should have said, he wants to see you *die*. By now he'll have us visual. In a few moments' time he'll have the pleasure of watching this plane explode in a cloud of flame. There's a bomb on board – and don't bother trying to find it: you won't. And now—'

David's foot lashed out and kicked her gun hand. The *crack* of the shot made Melanie's ears ring. By the time they had cleared, David had leaped out of his seat and was grappling with Abby. Melanie didn't pause to think. She released her belt and leaped up to help her husband.

Abby was a trained fighter but the two of them outweighed her. The three fell in a tight human knot. Both Melanie and David were trying to evade Abby's jabbing hands and elbows; David was clinging onto her gun hand. Melanie felt the lump of the hard drive through Abby's coat. Her fingers scrabbled for it and closed over the plastic casing.

'Got it!' David shouted. He sprang back clutching the gun. Melanie leaped away from Abby with the hard drive in her hand.

Abby lay on the floor of the cabin and glared at them. Then, abruptly, she laughed and jumped to her feet in one movement. 'Oh my. The big man has the gun. Better use it, then, hadn't you?'

She sauntered over to the locker at the end of the cabin and pulled out a parachute.

'Stop!' David ordered. He held the gun in both hands and aimed it at her.

Abby began to whistle a little tune as she shrugged the parachute harness over her shoulders.

David tightened his grip. Melanie couldn't help but notice that the aim wavered slightly. 'I said, *stop*!'

'Oh, did you? I didn't hear. Sorry.'

Abby fastened the buckles and moved swiftly to the door. 'You know,' she remarked over her shoulder, 'you could shoot at any time.' Then she turned to face them, holding her arms out. 'Here I am. You couldn't miss. Not that it would do you any good, because the bomb goes off with or without me. But you could get your revenge . . . Take me down with you . . .' A pause. 'But of course, you won't, because you're David Granger and you're one of the nice guys. And that, my friend, is why we will win and you will lose.'

She turned to the door and pulled on the fastening lever with both hands. The door swung into the cabin and let in a howling blast of freezing air. Abby shouted something over the noise: it might have been 'So long.' And then she was gone.

David staggered over against the gale and pushed the door shut. 'I couldn't do it,' he muttered. 'I won't bring myself down to her level. No, love, stay there.' Melanie had been about to come and help him. 'Sit down and buckle up. We might be landing very hard, very quickly.'

He made his way quickly to the cockpit and dropped into the pilot's seat, his hands already moving over the controls.

Melanie fastened her seatbelt. 'We should find that bomb!' she called to him.

'She said we wouldn't,' he answered without looking round. 'It'll be in the fuselage or the avionics bay – somewhere you can't get at from inside. Our only hope is to override the autopilot and bring the plane down before it goes off. Think happy thoughts, sweetheart.'

And then there was nothing to do but watch him press buttons and flick switches, trying to regain control of the plane.

Melanie sat back and closed her eyes, breathing

slowly to calm her racing heart. Happy thoughts? OK. That was easy.

Beck.

Their son. She pictured him as she had last seen him, face reluctantly upturned for a goodbye kiss. Her face, and David's dark hair.

Be brave, darling, she thought. *Be brave, be str—*

Chapter 1

The sun was rising over the Himalayas. Red light touched the very tops of the peaks and slowly flooded down mighty walls of snow and rock. It tumbled into the valleys and brought the world out of the dark.

Without the mountains in the way, it would have appeared much earlier. The small group – two boys and a man – had started walking an hour earlier when the world had been grey and shapeless. Now the sun had finally caught up with itself.

It was an awesome sight and Beck Granger took a moment to stand and watch.

'C'mon, Blondie.' James gave him a nudge as he walked by. The lanky teenager was a couple of years older than Beck, but even with his long legs he usually trailed behind by a good ten metres. James's lungs laboured in the thin air. He wasn't as fit as either Beck or Ian, and they were all carrying fully laden bergens – military-grade backpacks that were tough and waterproof and could hold almost anything.

'Keep moving, Beck,' Ian called from the front, sounding irritable. He was a stocky, powerful man with grizzled grey hair. The first time Beck had seen him, back in South Africa, he had thought of a silverback gorilla. He walked along as if the world had done something that really annoyed him, and he was taking it out on the ground. 'We can't delay.'

Beck hid his own irritation. At fourteen, he was the youngest of the three. Despite this, he was still the one who knew the most about surviving in the wild. But Ian, the adult who knew where they were going, couldn't get out of the habit of giving orders.

So Beck tore his gaze away to follow after their leader. 'So, this place we're going,' he called. 'We're on a schedule?'

Well, it was worth a try. Ian was being very tight-lipped about their destination. All Beck knew was that they were somewhere in the Nepalese Himalayas. Even Ian couldn't really disguise that fact. The big hills were the giveaway. But where in the Himalayas? And what were they going to do when they got there?

But Ian was used to keeping secrets. He didn't share. He didn't even look round, just kept trudging. 'We'll get there quicker if you don't stop to admire the view.'

Beck sighed again. He had been brought up to appreciate the sheer *awesomeness* of the world around him. And who wouldn't find the Himalayas amazing?

Apparently, Ian Bostock and James Blake wouldn't.

He glanced up at their backs as they walked. Ian and James were not the company he would ever have expected to be keeping as he trekked across the Himalayas.

The three of them looked like a normal group of European trekkers. If there was anything unusual about them, it was that they hadn't hired guides and porters from the Sherpas – the people who lived in the eastern regions of Nepal's mountains. But not all westerners did that. Apart from that, there was nothing about them to attract attention.

16

They wore sturdy, ankle-supporting boots; light-weight but strong trousers; and, on top, thin layers of T-shirts, sweatshirts and cagoules – stuff you could easily take off or put on as required, letting the air circulate and carry sweat away. They had to dress for all temperatures. The days started at freezing point but warmed up by the afternoon. At the moment they all wore woollen hats to keep the heat in their bodies. Before long, they would be in T-shirts.

However, looks were deceptive. There was nothing normal about them. Ian had been a trained killer. He had been the partner of Abby Blake, James's psychotic mother, until finally his conscience had got the better of him. And James was . . . ? Beck wondered how to describe James. An untrained killer? Or just a very messed-up young man? James's career as an assassin had been short and very unsuccessful, in that he hadn't assassinated anybody. It had turned out that he didn't have the stomach for it. As Beck had been the one James was meant to be assassinating, he was quite grateful for this.

Not that Beck's own circumstances were straightforward.

Beck was officially dead. It had been on all the news channels. He had become unusually famous – the boy who kept surviving – turning into a reluctant media personality, after years of keeping quiet and hidden. So when he apparently died, torn to pieces by wild dogs in the Kruger National Park, the media were all over it.

After viewing all the evidence that he and Ian had carefully faked, the authorities in South Africa had declared him dead. Green Force had checked this evidence – and they had some very suspicious lawyers – and had been convinced. Which meant that even his own Uncle Al believed it was true, though it broke Beck's heart to think how Al must have suffered.

All for one reason: to bring down Lumos.

Chapter 2

To the rest of the world, Lumos was a multinational energy company. Maybe it had a dodgy environmental track record, but that was in faraway places that no one cared about – except organizations like Green Force. But to Beck, Lumos was the monster that had plagued his life and killed his parents. Green Force was in a constant state of undeclared war with Lumos, and Beck was at the front line. If Lumos found out that he was alive, he very soon wouldn't be. They would certainly come after him. Edwin Blake, the head of Lumos and James's grandfather, was not a man to let bygones be bygones.

And so Beck had had to work hard to stay dead. Lumos's agents were everywhere, and so was CCTV. Software could scan recordings and pick out known faces. It could analyse body shape and the way you walked. Beck had had to change.

James had called him 'Blondie'. Beck's dark hair was dyed blond, and he had let it grow unusually long. Not long long, but certainly longer than he was used to. He had always kept it cut short, because with the life he led you wanted hair that could be washed quickly and easily in the nearest water source. Now, for the first time in his life, it had grown over his ears.

These precautions scarcely seemed enough when you thought of what the three of them were up against. A man and two boys against one of the world's largest, richest companies with its own private army of hired assassins . . . The odds against them seemed overwhelming.

And yet, as he trudged along the stony ground and the world grew light around him, Beck felt almost peaceful. It was strange to think that, all too soon, he would either have won or he would be really, truly dead. It was all coming to a head. Beck could sense it. Yet he still felt a calm descend on him.

Part of it was the coming day. The sky was turning into a blue dome above them from horizon to horizon.

They were walking over a rocky plateau, so high that in some cases they were looking down on the smaller mountain tops.

Part of it was a sense of freedom. There was no CCTV up here on the roof of the world. He could walk freely, and with a light heart.

And part of it was just being positive. His parents, and Uncle Al, and everyone who ever taught him the survival skills that had kept Beck alive, had advised him to maintain a positive mental attitude. Most boys his age hadn't experienced plane crashes, shipwrecks, erupting volcanoes . . . If any had seen a tiger or a poisonous snake, then it had been in a zoo, not at such close quarters that the slightest mistake could kill them. He had been threatened by drug lords, Arctic storms, illegal loggers, poachers, and he had survived all those threats by never giving up. It had made him who he was today – a survivor. So he wasn't going to give in to negative thinking now, and he would enjoy the beauty of the Himalayas while he could.

Ian held his hand up – the sign that they should stop. In front of him the ground vanished.

Beck came forward and peered over the drop. Way, way below was a valley. The floor was carpeted with green fields. In winter it would be thick with snow, but now, in the summer, the snow was confined to the higher altitudes above them. It was a long way down.

Even Beck, who didn't usually suffer from vertigo, had to take a grip on himself and step carefully away from the edge.

James had gone green. 'You're going to say we have to get down there, aren't you?' he said faintly.

Ian grinned like a wolf. 'Yup.' He rubbed his hands together. 'That's exactly what I'm going to say.'

Chapter 3

'Whoa! I'm falling!'

Beck flinched as loose pebbles and grit tumbled past his face.

James slithered down the rock face towards him before he somehow got a grip and stopped. He peered down at Beck. 'Sorry . . .'

Beck rolled his eyes and smiled.

The sheer slope had nothing to break your fall. So if one teenage boy didn't hold on properly, he had enough weight and momentum to knock anyone else below him – say, another teenage boy and a grown man – off the rock and carry them with him. All the way down until the ground stopped them, *ker-splat*. 'Sorry' didn't really cover it.

But, hey, he told himself, he and Ian knew all this

off by heart. They needed James to learn it fast. James was a quick learner; just not always quick enough. In order to learn the right way, all too often he had to try the wrong way once.

'You're moving too quickly,' Beck said. 'There's no hurry. You've got two hands and two feet, so you're attached to the rock in four places. Just move one at a time. Never move two at the same time. Slowly does it, step by step. Climb on down beside me. We'll do it together.'

''Kay.' James started moving again, slowly and more carefully. After another minute he was next to Beck, clinging to the face of a mountain. He flashed Beck a grateful smile.

'Get a move on,' came an irritable call from below. It kind of contradicted Beck's assertion that there was no hurry. 'Plenty of time to rest when you're dead.'

'Well, there's a cheerful thought,' James muttered.

Beck glanced down. 'We can do it. That ledge there, see? Move your left foot down to it . . . OK, stop. Now let go with your right hand, move it along to that bulge there . . .'

It was like operating James by remote control, but they soon got the hang of it. Before long they were climbing down, side by side, slightly faster and a lot more safely than when James had been working it out on his own.

Even when he was babysitting James, Beck found climbing easy enough to devote other parts of his mind to other matters. Like keeping track of where they were going.

Ian had refused to tell them the plan, saying they would know when they needed to know. He had worked for Lumos, and if you were going to survive in Lumos, then you had to learn to keep secrets. Beck recognized that.

But it didn't make it any easier.

Back in South Africa, Ian had given Beck reason to trust him. He had saved his life and then put his neck on the line by helping fake his death, and then lying about it to Edwin Blake. He had got them this far without detection.

The three of them had made their way north and east, up Africa and through Asia, country by country. They had stayed in safe houses known to Ian from his former life. A few days ago they had reached the Indian border in a hired truck and slipped over it into the most south-eastern corner of Nepal, with Beck and James hidden under the floor. They had bounced along uncomfortably for a couple of hours before reaching their destination: a cabin perched high on a precipice somewhere. James and Beck had been left alone for forty-eight hours, with enough food to keep them going and a TV with movies to watch, but no means of communication with the outside world or learning where they were. Ian had returned with trekking supplies, and the next morning they had set out, on foot. That was yesterday. They had walked all day and spent the night in a tent. And now they were still walking. All Beck knew was that they were heading into the heart of Nepal.

But in spite of all this he still didn't feel he could fully trust Ian. Beck went along with him because Ian seemed to have a plan. But Beck also realized that Ian might be so good at keeping secrets that he was even fooling himself. So Beck kept a track of their surroundings as they went. Just in case. He might need to make a getaway on his own at some point . . .

Chapter 4

After half an hour of descending they reached a ledge on the side of the mountain. It was half the size of a tennis court, big enough to walk about on. On the other side was a drop that was even more sheer than the one they had just climbed down.

'And about time,' Ian announced as their feet touched the rock. 'Breakfast break. C'mon, chop chop. Beck, you've got the stove. James, you've got the food.'

Ian had most of the climbing gear and the tent in his bergen. Beck had the rest of the gear and the cooking equipment. James had the food. The boys swung their bulky bergens down onto the ground. Beck pulled out a canister of water and a small metal kettle, and the stove. It was a contraption like a metal grasshopper. He set it on the ground and hunted in his bergen for matches. The gas hissed, then lit with a comforting *whoomph*. Before long the air above the small circle of blue flame was shimmering with heat. He filled the metal kettle and set it on top to boil.

Meanwhile James was going through the food supplies – plastic packets with lettering in English and Nepalese. Beck made a mental note of how much food Ian had made them bring. It was another clue to how long they would be walking. Beck estimated that there was a couple of days' supply.

'Instant noodles and tahr,' James said. 'For a change.'

Beck smiled. Their food was samey, but it was good. A tahr was a goat-like animal. Its dried meat was tangy, with lots of energy.

James peered into a crumpled paper bag that Ian had bought at a Sherpa shack the day before. 'And what's this?'

Beck grinned. 'Himalayan candy!'

'Now you're talking!' James's face lit up as he plunged his hand into the bag. He plucked out something that looked very much like a yellow cube of solid wax. His face slowly fell. 'Uh, Beck . . .'

'It's cheese,' Beck told him.

'Cheese.'

'Hard dried yak cheese.'

James said nothing.

They had passed yaks along the way, being herded by their human masters. They were like cows but the size of carthorses. Thick pelts kept them warm even at the highest altitudes. Curved pointed horns as wide as Beck's outstretched arms made them look very dangerous, but they were placid animals. They could pull carts and ploughs; they could be ridden; and they provided meat and milk.

Beck took a piece for himself. 'See, they take the milk and turn it into cheese, and then they let it harden. One lump can last all day.'

James tapped his lump cautiously against a rock. It sounded just like two stones hitting each other. 'I can see why.'

'You don't chew it 'cos you'd break a tooth. Just suck it. For hours.'

They added boiling water to a saucepan of instant noodles and had a cup of tea to go with it. The food and drink left a comfortable warm glow inside them. It was like a boiler in Beck's stomach, sending energy to the rest of his body.

Ian kept himself to himself while Beck and James chatted about nothing much, which wasn't unusual. But Beck noticed him turn away, pulling something like a phone out of his pocket. For a moment Beck thought Ian must be going to check his route plan or something – but no, he had insisted that all phones be switched off and left behind so there wasn't the slightest chance of them being traced.

Ian then held up a crumpled piece of paper next to the screen. His eyes darted from one to the other. Beck leaned over casually. Ian had written what looked like a set of coordinates, and now Beck could see that the gadget in his hand was actually a GPS device.

Ian nodded to himself in satisfaction. He looked up to the horizon and absentmindedly made a chopping gesture with his hand. Beck's heart pounded. Was that where they were heading? It had to be. He scanned the horizon quickly. All he could see was mountains, but hey, he had a direction. He did his best to fix some of them in his head as landmarks.

He slid his hand into his pocket and pulled out a GPS of his own. It was a sturdy traveller's model, sealed in a thick rubber case. He craned his neck again for another glimpse of the figures on Ian's bit of paper so that he could enter them into his own device.

Ian looked up and scowled. He stuffed the paper into his pocket and switched off the GPS with a jab. 'I didn't know you had one of those.'

Beck shrugged. 'You didn't ask. I just want to know where we're going . . .'

'And I keep telling you, you kids don't need to know! The less you know, the more you can't tell anyone if we're caught.'

Beck felt his temper begin to flare. He didn't like being dismissed as a kid. He had helped keep both James and Ian alive while an army of poachers hunted for them. He was owed a bit more than this. However, he managed to keep a firm lid on his anger. 'We're putting a lot of faith in you—' he began.

Ian shot to his feet. 'Listen,' he barked back. 'You don't need to know a thing, *kid*, not one thing.' He jabbed a thumb at his powerful chest. '*I'm* the one putting everything on the line, got that? I had a career. I had a life. I'm sacrificing it all for two teenage boys.' He looked at James, who blushed and looked away. 'Correction: one teenage boy – and his friend. I promised Abby I'd keep James safe, and I keep my promises. James wants to get out of the family business? Fine, I'll help him, and the only way to do that is to bring the business down. So I'm doing it. I could do it all on my own – I could have left you two behind in Johannesburg – except that then I wouldn't be looking after James, would I? So James has to come with me, and that unfortunately means you have to come with me, and so I get to babysit the pair of you. That's the only reason you're here, kid. Meanwhile the plan, the way we're going to bring down Lumos – that is my responsibility alone. Got it? *Mine*.' His voice dropped to a mumble. 'Jeez, ten years in the Paras and I end up a nursemaid . . .'

And he turned and stormed off to the other end of the ledge.

Chapter 5

'Don't be angry with him.'

James said it softly, and Beck looked up in surprise. James usually went out of his way not to take sides. When he was little, it had always been assumed that he would one day take over Lumos. What that meant now was that James did his best not to be in charge of anything. He was happy to take orders from Beck or Ian. If Beck and Ian disagreed, he generally just melted into the background until the argument was over.

Beck glanced over to where Ian was pacing about, as far away from them as it was possible to get without flying. 'I'm not angry. I just don't understand him.'

'Yeah, well, I've known him longer than you.'

James shifted into a more comfortable position. They were sitting cross-legged on cold, hard rock. 'He's like this 'cos he's scared.'

'*Scared?*' Beck looked at Ian again.

Ian was the man who had tracked him across the African veld, relentlessly and successfully. He had engaged in a gunfight with poachers who would have killed him without a thought. He had faced down a pack of African wild dogs. For goodness' sake, he had been Abby Blake's partner! If that wasn't terrifying, then what was?

'Of what Lumos might do to him?' he said.

'Nah, not that. He's not fussed about little things like dying. What really scares him is failure. He's never been good at that. No one at Lumos is. And' – James leaned closer and lowered his voice – 'I think he may be a little lost.'

Beck groaned. 'Oh, great!'

'But he'll figure it out,' James added hastily. 'Eventually. And look, everything he was saying about only bringing you along because he had to bring me . . . that's rubbish. Face it. If he hadn't really wanted to bring us, he'd have found a safe place to leave us. We just have to trust that he'll explain himself in time.'

Ian came striding back along the ledge. 'Drink up and pack up. We move on in five minutes.'

He rummaged inside his own bag, then pulled out a coil of orange climbing rope, as thick as a finger. Beck guessed it was a fifty-metre length. He also pulled out a smaller bag that clinked metallically when he set it down on the rock. By the time Beck had folded up the stove and stashed it in his bergen, Ian had produced a second fifty-metre coil and shaken their harnesses out. The harnesses were like pairs of shorts after a severe moth attack had eaten away all the fabric. There was a strong band that went around the waist, with dangling loops that the legs went through.

Ian and Beck climbed easily into theirs, and then had to help James get his straightened out.

Beck felt James trembling as he looked down the slope they were about to descend. ''s OK,' he murmured. 'We can do this together, right?'

James shot him a nervous glance.

'Together,' Beck repeated.

Meanwhile Ian was laying out the rope, freeing any tangles that had crept in while it was in his bergen. He tied the ends of the two coils together with a deft, smooth flick of the wrist. From the bottom of the bergen he produced two metal bolts and a small metal hammer. He began to walk along the ledge, eyes scanning the rock at his feet. Then he dropped down abruptly by a small crack and used the hammer to drive the bolts into the rock.

'Beck, talk James through how abseiling works. I'm guessing you've done this before.'

'Yeah, once or twice . . .'

Beck delved into the small bag and held up a steel loop. One side of it was hinged so that he could snap it open and shut with his thumb. 'This is a carabiner, and it goes here.' He snapped it onto a buckle at the front of James's harness. Then he held up a piece of metal like a figure of eight – two solid loops stuck together, one larger than the other. 'And this is a descender.' He snapped it onto the carabiner and then screwed a small metal sleeve over the carabiner's hinge to lock it tight. He proceeded to demonstrate by sticking his fingers through the loops of the descender. 'The rope goes through these loops, and that creates friction, which slows you down. You hold the rope above the descender with your right hand. That's your guide hand. Your left hand is your brake hand. I'll also tie an autoblock for you. That's a knot that wraps around the rope below the descender. You keep your brake hand on the autoblock. If you accidentally let go of it, it automatically wraps tight around the rope and holds it fast. That means you stop.'

'So,' James said slowly, 'I'm trusting my life to one thin rope?'

Beck grinned. 'Yup!'

'That'll take some getting used to . . .'

Chapter 6

Ian had hammered both bolts securely into the rock. He attached a carabiner to each one, then ran the doubled-up rope through them. A couple of sharp tugs satisfied him that the bolts weren't going to budge. He fastened a descender to his own harness and threaded the double strands of the rope through the loops, as Beck had described to James. Beck watched as he tied on his own autoblock. It was a thin loop of red nylon cord, which Ian wrapped four or five times around the rope. He spoke as he was doing this:

'I'll go first. James comes second, so Beck can check his knots for him and I can look out for him from below. Beck comes down last. Once we're all down, I'll give the rope a tug, it'll slide through and come down after us. Then we do the next stretch.'

He arranged the autoblock carefully so that all the wraps on the rope were neatly stacked, one on top of the other, and not tangled or criss-crossing. Then he clipped both ends of the remaining cord to a second carabiner on his harness.

'Questions?'

'Uh . . .' Beck glanced at the bolts and the carabiners in them. 'We won't be coming back this way?'

'Don't plan to. Why?'

'So we don't come back for the bolts?'

On climbing routes that were frequently used, it was quite usual to leave bolts attached for the next climbers. But when it came to climbing on fresh rock that had never been used before, like here, Beck had always been taught that you tidied up after yourself. In his eyes, leaving those metal bolts was almost like littering. His Green Force upbringing just made him want to say *no*!

Ian didn't seem to understand his concern. 'We've got enough bolts and carabiners for four descents, and that'll put us right where we're meant to be. We'll be on a route that'll take us straight to Lumos without anyone seeing us.'

Four descents, Beck thought. The two ropes together, doubled up, were fifty metres. So, four descents of fifty metres was 200 metres. Quite a drop. But they were still a lot more than 200 metres above the valley floor. He remembered what James had said about Ian maybe being lost . . .

He pushed the thought away. He had even less idea of where they were than Ian did. He just had to trust the man.

Ian picked up the rope as Beck had described to James – right hand above the descender, left hand at waist level holding the autoblock below. He turned his back on the sheer drop and walked backwards to the edge.

'Be seeing you!'

And then he was gone. The rope tugged and jerked in its bolts under Ian's weight. Thirty seconds later it went limp.

'OK,' came the call from below. Beck pulled the rope up for James to use.

'Don't look down,' James was muttering. 'Don't look down . . .'

'You'll be fine. Keep a wide stance and be confident. Trust gravity!' Beck grinned.

'*Do not* mention *gravity* to me *ever again*,' James muttered.

Beck winked as he ran the rope through James's descender and tied an autoblock for him.

James went on, 'I can't believe I'm about to do this. You know, I'd never thought about the expression "thin air" before. What's so thin about air? I'll tell you: it can't support any weight, that's what, and I'm going down through it . . .'

'You'll be fine,' Beck said again. 'The bolts are solid, the rope's solid, the autoblock is your back-up – it's impossible to fall.'

'Did you know that the laws of physics say it's impossible for a bumblebee to fly?' James said. 'Problem is, no one ever told the bumblebees . . .'

But for all his grumbling, James was doing as he was told and getting into position.

Beck knew from experience that grumbling and muttering were his friend's way of mustering courage. 'Let the rope run smoothly through your brake hand as you go . . .'

'And grip tight to stop. Got it. Supposing the friction burns my fingers?'

'Then you're going too fast,' Beck said with a smile.

'Ha ha. OK, here goes nothing.'

James went down with a lot less grace than Ian, stepping backwards slowly and working his way nervously down the cliff. Beck craned his neck over to follow his progress. 'Good job, James. Looking strong,' he called reassuringly.

After a couple of minutes the rope went limp again. The call came from below for Beck to come down. He pulled the rope back up, fastened it to his descender and kicked himself away from the cliff.

Chapter 7

The rope ran smoothly through Beck's fingers. The rock face ran up past his eyes as though he was going down in an elevator. Thirty seconds later he was on a ledge with James and Ian.

It was much smaller than the last one – barely five metres in length and as wide as a man's outstretched arms. James was standing well away from the edge, his back pressed to the rock. In front was nothing but thin air, and then the sheer rock of the mountains on the other side of the valley.

Beck winced when he saw that Ian was already hammering in a fresh set of bolts.

'Get the rope down, Beck?'

The rope was doubled up. Beck pulled on one strand. The other end ran up and out of sight above them. It passed through the bolts on the ledge they had come from, and a moment later came tumbling down again. Beck began to coil it up while Ian got ready for the next stage. He was checking his GPS against his bit of paper again.

'Bang on course,' he announced gruffly.

'Good,' James said. He tilted his head back and looked up the way they had come. ''Cos I'd hate to have to climb back up.'

Ian put the GPS and paper away. 'Three more descents and we're on a track that we can just walk down. We've shaved a whole day off our journey, coming this way.'

Beck peered over the edge. The rock bulged out below them, so it was impossible to see what lay underneath. 'You're sure?' he asked. He couldn't see what was ahead, and that made him nervous. He liked to know what he was getting into.

Ian scowled as he began to fit the rope to his descender. 'Positive. Right, same as before – me, James, Beck. You getting the hang of it, James?'

James beamed. 'Yeah. Prepared. Set.'

'Then here we go . . .'

Ian backed his way down the bulge of rock, rope running between his fingers, and dropped out of sight. The boys waited for the sign that he had reached the next level below them.

And waited.

And waited some more.

They exchanged glances. Beck checked the rope. It was still rigid, so Ian's weight was still on the other end. And it was still quivering, which meant that Ian was moving about below. But surely he must have made the maximum fifty metres by now . . .

Finally the call came from below: 'OK . . .' Beck strained his ears. Did Ian actually sound uncertain? That wasn't like him.

But what else could 'OK' mean? The rope was limp; Beck could now get James fastened up.

'See you on the other side!' James said with a grin, and kicked his way backwards off the ledge with a new-found confidence.

Almost immediately Beck heard his panicked yelp:

'Whoa! No! Oops. Help!'

Beck tried to look over the jutting lip of rock, but

it obscured the two figures. He strained to listen. It sounded like Ian was shouting encouragement or instructions from below. Beck tried to tell himself that James must have hit the sort of trouble that any newbie could get into. Probably managed to get himself upside down. Ian seemed to be sorting it out.

After an eternity, the call came for Beck to follow. Beck fastened himself onto the rope and backed over the bulge.

He saw immediately why James had been having issues. The bulge was an overhang. He was dangling vertically and his feet had nothing to push against. James had been trying to walk down the rock face, like he had the first time. That was why he had got into difficulties. He wasn't experienced enough to do what Beck now did – which was just let himself run down the rope. He didn't make any contact with the rock until his boots touched down next to his companions.

But where he stopped wasn't a ledge. It was just the top of another rocky bulge. All three of them had to brace to avoid sliding down the slope. Anything they put down would just roll away over the edge.

James was staring at Beck; he looked slightly green. Ian's face was set and hard, the way it went when he had to share bad news.

Beck frowned. 'What?'

Ian actually swallowed and coughed. 'I, uh, miscalculated. But only a little.'

'Look at the next descent,' James said faintly.

Cautiously Beck leaned out and looked down. His heart turned to ice.

He was looking down a sheer drop. There had to be 200 metres of air between them and the next rocky slope. There were no ledges anywhere in between. Nowhere to rest for three abseilers with fifty metres of rope – or even 100 metres, if they used the full length.

Beck felt anger surge up inside him. 'You let us climb down when you knew we were just getting into a dead end?'

Climbing back up that overhang would be next to impossible. A skilled climber could potentially do it, with the right equipment and a degree of luck. He, Beck, could maybe do it. Someone like James would never get up there.

'So what do we do?' James asked, almost in a whisper. He craned his neck to look back the way they had come.

A thousand tons of rock hung over them. They had climbed themselves down into a death trap.

Chapter 8

'Can we climb back up?' James asked in panicky tones.

'Of course we don't climb up,' Ian said irritably. 'I wouldn't have let you both come down if we were doing that. We climb along.'

'Along?' Beck asked.

Ian edged a little further along the bulge where they stood and pointed. The slope grew steeper, but it wasn't as sheer as the drop below. No one could walk on it, but someone clinging on with both hands and feet could make their way along it. Most of it.

After about fifty metres, the slope curved away out of sight round the mountain. Below it, Beck couldn't help noticing, the drop was just as vertical.

'We can climb along there,' Ian said. 'Just a bit

further round the corner, and then it'll be flat enough to climb back up.'

'So, uh, why didn't we come down that way in the first place?' James asked. He flushed when Ian shot him a sharp look, but didn't look away. Even James was asking Ian questions, Beck thought – the situation had to be bad.

'Because, there, I knew that, if we came down that way, we would end up over a sharp drop,' Ian said through gritted teeth. 'Here, I thought we would make it. I was wrong. I'm sorry. Hey, don't worry. We'll be tied together.'

'Why?' James muttered. 'So if one of us falls, we all fall?'

'So if one of us falls there's two people holding him, anchored to the rock,' Ian corrected. He turned back to Beck. 'Spring-loaded cams, three of 'em, bottom right pocket.'

Beck delved into Ian's bergen and produced a handful of gadgets the size of his wrist. James looked at them with interest. They looked like random collections of semicircular blades joined together.

'You talk him through using these while I get the rope ready,' Ian instructed.

Beck held up one of the devices and pressed his thumb against a switch. James recoiled as the blades suddenly sprang apart.

'Each of us will have one of these,' Beck said. 'It'll be attached to our harnesses. You jam it into a crack in the rock and press the switch. The blades open up like that and they hold firm. So you can't fall.'

'I'll go first,' Ian said as he fastened the rope to his harness, then to James's, then to Beck's. There was about fifteen metres of rope between each of them. The rest of it was coiled around Ian's shoulder. 'I'll go out as far as I can and use my cam to hold on. James, you come out to join me and hold on with yours. I go a bit further. Then Beck comes out to join you, then you move . . . and so on. At any point, two of us will be fastened to the rock and we'll all be tied together.' He pinched James's pale cheek. 'See? Safe!'

And James would be in the middle, supported at either end by two experienced climbers, Beck thought. It was a good plan. And it was their only hope.

Chapter 9

James mumbled something like ''Kay.'

Beck helped him to find a good place to stick his cam into the rock. Then Ian sidled across the sharp slope, swiftly and confidently. He got out about ten metres and called over for James.

'Remember what I said?' Beck reminded him. 'Only move one limb at a time. Keep the others firmly planted.'

'If I don't leave finger holes in the rock, it'll be a miracle,' James promised.

Beck showed him how to disengage his cam one final time, and made sure that his own was securely fastened. Then James began fumbling his way out towards Ian. James was a lot slower. He felt his way with his feet, rather than looking down to place them. Looking down would have meant taking in the abyss beneath him. Beck could see his legs shaking, but James was biting his lip and forcing himself to go on. It took about five minutes for him to reach Ian.

Ian patted him on the shoulder. 'Way to go. That gap there – see? Stick your cam in there . . .'

Beck heard the comforting *snick* of a cam opening.

'That's it. Right, I'll go on a bit more, then Beck comes out to join us. You can't fall . . .'

Ian detached his own cam and continued across, leaving James stranded like a fly clinging to a wall. James kept his eyes fixed firmly on the rock a few centimetres in front of him. Ian climbed along to the full extent of his rope and latched himself onto the rock again. Now it was Beck's turn to detach his cam and climb out to join James. There was something final about it, he thought. All three of them were now clinging to the rock over the sheer 200-metre drop.

'Hi there,' he said conversationally as he approached. He jammed his cam into the rock next to James's. 'Haven't we met somewhere before?'

'Yeah, the face is familiar.' James's chin was quivering but he forced a brave smile.

'The name's Beck. I'd shake hands but, you know . . .' Beck rolled his eyes. 'Climbing.'

James actually laughed, though it was more like a sharp expulsion of breath.

Beck peered past him. 'You know, there's a guy over there – bad-tempered ex-Para sort – I think he'd really like you to go and join him.'

'Oh, well, if he insists. I'd love to stay and chat but, you know . . .' James forced a smile.

'I understand. My Uncle Al says we should always respect our elders and betters.'

James set off towards Ian. He was moving a lot better now, Beck noted.

And so the three of them made their way, one by one, across the cliff face. Beck was pleased by James's increasing sureness. He still kept a close eye on his friend to check that he wasn't getting *too* confident. That was how mistakes got made. He could tell that Ian was doing the same from the other side.

They had climbed round the curve of the mountain

now. The ledge they had abseiled down to was out of sight. Ahead, past James and Ian, Beck could see a spur of rock jutting out. Above it the slope was much less steep. They were almost there – they could get onto that spur, make their way back to the top, and find another way down.

Beck and James were both fastened to the rock and it was Ian's turn to go. He was about five metres from the spur when they heard a *crack* and a rumble from above. All three of them jerked their heads up.

A cluster of small rocks came tumbling down towards them. They bounced and spun almost lazily in the air, like they were made of feathers or falling in low gravity.

'Hold on!' Ian yelled, and then the rocks were upon them and there was nothing light about them at all. Beck pressed himself into the cliff face, but they weren't falling on him. One of them struck James's bergen a glancing blow, but not enough to dislodge him.

And one of them struck Ian square on the shoulder. With a sharp cry, he was dashed off the cliff. He fell into the abyss, stopping short as his rope jerked, all his weight now on James's small rock cam device.

James yelled as the taut rope forced him against the rock face. Ian was spinning on the rope that came straight down from his harness, tight as a drum.

'*It's not going to hold!*' James screamed. Already the cam was shifting out of the crack it was fixed into. James's whole body trembled as he clung there, spread-eagled flat against the rock. Beck could see that he was holding on with every ounce of strength.

'My shoulder . . .' Ian groaned. 'I think it's broken . . .'

'*Pull yourself up!*' James's voice shook with panic. His eyes were screwed tight shut, his face ground into the rock. '*Pull yourself up! I don't know how long the cam will hold . . .*'

The cam was now secured by just two teeth and was on the verge of popping out.

Ashen-faced, Beck looked down at Ian. Ian met his eyes and a silent understanding passed between them. They had seconds in which to act, no more. The cam's grip would never hold two of them.

With his good hand, Ian dug a knife out of his

belt and held it up for Beck to see. Even then, Beck hoped against hope that he was going to do something clever with it. Jam it into the rock, use it as a foot support . . .

But no.

'I'm sorry, James, mate. I did my best. You're a good lad.'

The finality in his voice pierced the panic that gripped James's mind. *What? Wait!*

Ian gave Beck a final look as he brought the blade up to the rope. 'Beck. Remember this.' He rattled off a stream of figures – coordinates for a GPS. 'Repeat that back to me.'

Beck did so, though his throat was dry and he could barely get the words out; he had to raise his voice over James's gabbled questions.

'And when you get there,' Ian ordered, 'find Sangmu.'

'Who—' Beck began as Ian pressed the blade against the rope. It parted almost instantly.

Ian tumbled away into the air, shrinking in a second to a figure the size of a doll. His voice echoed up from below: *Sangmu!*

And then it was drowned out by James's heartbroken shriek of grief as he realized what Ian had done.

Beck pressed his face into the rock so that he couldn't see Ian hit the ground. But they both heard the loud thump from far below.

Chapter 10

Beck took several long, shuddering breaths to calm his racing heart. Then he climbed along the rock to James.

James's whole body shook with sobs. 'I did it, I killed him, I'm so stupid I can't even attach a simple stupid cam properly – I killed him . . .'

Beck dug his own cam into the rock and, awkwardly, put his hand on James's shoulder. It was all he could do. He hadn't known Ian well; he couldn't have called the man a friend. The sudden death was a shock, but that was only natural. Beck knew he would get over it. But James had known Ian very well indeed.

He looked up to where James's cam had been. A small crater of fresh rock, lighter than the rest, had opened up. The cam had pulled it open. 'Your cam was fine,' he said. 'It was the rock that was bad. Don't blame yourself.'

Beck grabbed the cam that dangled from James's harness and jammed it into a new crack, testing it with a tug. Now at least they were both properly fastened.

James's sobs slowly died away. He stared fixedly at the rock wall. His chest rose and fell with slow, deliberate breaths. He showed no sign of moving.

Beck squeezed the hand that was on his shoulder. 'We should keep going.'

James didn't take his eyes off the rock. 'Why?' he said hoarsely.

Beck hesitated. 'Because if we don't, eventually we'll fall,' he said.

'Maybe I want to fall.'

Beck thought about it. The attraction of just being dead, when everything seemed lost . . . Then he thought about everything he loved – Uncle Al, his friend Peter, the adventures he still had ahead of him – so much to do, so many places to see. No, he had to stay alive. None of that would happen if he lay cold and smashed at the bottom of a mountain.

'Nah,' he said. 'We're going to finish this.'

A pause.

'Yes, we are,' James whispered back.

Beck gave his shoulder a final squeeze and took his hand away.

'And in case you were forgetting, I've had to deal with this before,' James added.

It took Beck a moment to realize what James meant. Not that long ago, James had lost his mother. Ian had been like a father to him, and now he was gone too.

Beck knew from experience that you never got over losing your parents. Al had done his best to replace them, and Green Force had been almost like a family. But it wasn't the same.

What you did do was learn to live with it.

'I know,' Beck replied quietly.

James released his cam and moved off without a backward glance. Beck waited until he was securely fixed five metres away, then followed.

Five minutes later they were safely on the rock spur they had been aiming for. They could stand without need for cams or ropes. Beck slowly coiled up the remains of the rope and stowed it in his bergen. They had about fifteen metres, give or take. The rest had gone down with Ian. Not a word passed between them as they started to trudge back up the slope.

Twenty minutes later they were back at the top.

James sat on the rock with his head in his hands. 'That's it, then. We're finished. We don't know where we're going. And look at us – two boys! We can't take on Lumos by ourselves.' His voice began to rise. 'Do you know how big it is? How powerful? We're just kids! And we don't know where we are or where we're going . . .'

Beck sensed a panic attack heading James's way. It would arrive in about a minute, and after that James would be good for nothing.

'*I just want to go home!*' James howled.

Beck squatted down in front of him and looked him in the eye. Now, he decided, James was ready for the big picture.

'Too late,' he snapped. 'And it's been too late ever since we decided to do this. Ever since I agreed to play dead. Go home? Sure. Right. Then what? It will take Lumos about two and a half seconds to find me and finish me. And probably you too, for good measure.'

James stared at him, face ashen with shock. Beck was right.

'Remember who had this idea in the first place? Who first thought we could do this?' Beck softened his voice and gave James a gentle poke in the chest. '*You* did. It was your plan and it's a darn good one. Me, I like being alive, I like being in the world – but the world would be a whole lot better off without Lumos in it. We can do this.'

James looked at him. 'How?'

Beck dug out his GPS and quickly tapped the coordinates Ian had shouted out into it. He kept talking while he waited for it to go through its locating routine.

'Ian gave us that clue: Sangmu.' He saw James's questioning look. 'I don't know – a place? A person? Someone's cat? We'll find out. We know the direction we were headed, and judging by the supplies we brought with us, our destination can't be more than a couple of days away.'

Beck straightened up and followed the route of the ridge with his eyes. They shouldn't have tried to climb down anywhere along here. They should have pressed on for at least another mile, maybe more, to avoid that sheer 200-metre drop.

'It looks like, if we follow the ridge, it starts to drop down. That should get us past the cliff. After that we can probably find another way down into the valley.'

James followed his gaze, and his shoulders sagged. Then he shrugged, clambered slowly to his feet and began to walk. 'I guess we better get on with it, then.'

Beck smiled and squeezed James's shoulder as he began to follow on behind.

Chapter 11

It took the rest of the day to make their way down from the high ground.

They had to proceed carefully, to make sure they didn't climb themselves down into another trap. They walked for another hour before Beck spotted what looked like a manageable route. It went out along the top of a spur, giving a good view of the way down in all directions. From there Beck could plan the rest of the descent. There were slopes on all sides; he chose the one with the gentlest gradient. The way was still rocky and littered with scree – broken fragments of rock that had come tumbling down over the centuries. They had to walk carefully, judging each step as they planted their boots amidst the loose stones. It was difficult and jarring on the legs.

Every footfall was a little lower than the last, which put added strain on their knees and thigh muscles. Beck knew from experience that walking uphill might tire the leg muscles more, but coming down was always tougher on the body. They kept their knees bent to absorb the impact of each step, though it made the thigh muscles complain loudly in protest at the extra work.

Apart from the occasional grunt or muttered request, they were silent. James was just walking on autopilot. He could put one foot in front of another, and leave the rest to his body while his mind assimilated the tragedy that had happened. Beck felt sad as well – not just because of the sudden, shocking loss of Ian, but also for James, who had lost everyone he had ever been close to.

Except me, Beck thought. He would be there for James. Despite James's Lumos past, they were friends for good. And friends stick together. Through thick and thin.

It was hard to say precisely when they made the transition from mountain to valley, but as they lost altitude, the land slowly changed colour. The slopes that had been bare and rocky became lush and green. Below them, terraced fields rose up from the valley floor. Above the fields the slopes were thickly wooded with conifers. Rhododendron bushes the size of houses dotted the green, like someone had shaken a brush over the valley and splattered it with red.

The temperature rose as they dropped down. When they entered the trees it grew distinctly humid. Beck estimated it was a good twenty degrees. Air that had been crisp and clear in the mountains was suddenly scented with pine resin and mulch. The sky was a vivid blue above them and the sun was bright, sending dazzling rays down through the branches. It wasn't long before their cagoules and top layers had disappeared into their bergens, and they marched along in T-shirts and sunglasses.

James suddenly spoke, though his voice was still flat and lifeless.

'You don't think of trees and Nepal. You think of mountains and snow. That's all you see on TV.'

'I read that in 2014 in Kathmandu, two thousand people each hugged a tree for World Environment

Day,' Beck said. 'It was a world record.' He looked sideways at James to see if there was any sign of amusement. 'So, there's at least two thousand trees.'

James's lips moved in a quick flash of a smile. 'Or one really big one.' His mouth settled back into a straight line.

They emerged from the trees and saw terraces spread out before them. Here they finally saw a few people about – Sherpa herders and farmers heading home along tracks on either side of the river. None of them spotted the two boys.

They were much further south than in England, so night came quickly. The valley was already in shadow. For the same reason you didn't see the sunrise until later, the sun disappeared from the sky even earlier than it would on flat ground. The mountains obscured its descent.

Beck checked the GPS, then pointed ahead, to where a rocky ridge bulged out of the side of the valley. 'We'll make our way past that point and then find a place to camp,' he said. But then he remembered that Ian had been carrying the camping gear. It would be a cold night ahead of them.

By the time they came to the place Beck had pointed out, they were completely alone. Not a soul around for miles, which suited Beck fine.

When he called a halt, James simply stopped and shucked his bergen onto the ground. 'Here, I suppose? It's south-facing.'

Beck was pleased to hear this. A remark like that showed that the old James was still there – buried under the shock of losing Ian, but still there. There had been a time when James was Beck's greatest fan (as well as wanting to kill him). He had read up on all the survival tips he could find, and he knew that, because the sun moved from east to west via the south, anything that was south-facing got the sun's heat for most of the day. The warmth would linger.

Unfortunately that was only part of the picture.

'True,' he said. 'But we're also surrounded by mountains.'

James put his hands on his hips and stared around as if noticing the Himalayas for the first time. 'Good grief. Why was I not informed?' He cocked a sideways look at Beck, and now there was definitely a smile. It even lasted longer than a second. The old James was coming back.

'Cold air sinks,' Beck said, 'and it will come tumbling down the mountains to the bottom of the valley. This whole area could freeze.'

James groaned. 'So we go back up?'

'Not far. We basically want a piece of flat – flattish – ground about thirty metres above the valley bottom. It'll be a good couple of degrees warmer.'

'South-facing,' James added, defending his one item of knowledge.

Beck nodded. 'And preferably protected by heat-absorbing trees or rocks.'

'With en-suite bathroom and maid service.'

'Well, naturally. Goes without saying.'

James grabbed his bergen and they trudged back up the slope. 'Or we might find a cave?' he said hopefully.

'We might.' Beck hated to let him down when he was trying to contribute ideas. 'But if we can find it, someone else will have found it first. Probably someone with teeth and claws. And the whole place will be one big en-suite bathroom. Floor and walls covered with droppings. And it will be cold and damp.'

'OK,' James replied after a pause, 'let's not try and find a cave.' He stayed silent for a moment as they kept walking. 'Um. Teeth and claws . . . Just what kind of animals are we talking about?'

Beck thought. 'Of the toothy and clawy variety . . . Tigers. Leopards. Wolves. Bears . . .'

Chapter 12

James's eyes went wide and round. He peered around and up into the trees as if expecting an attack by a marauding pack of predators.

'Most of those will be up in the mountains,' Beck said quickly. 'And more are endangered.'

'What's so great about being endangered?'

'Means they're rare so we probably won't meet them . . . Hey, here's a place.'

They were just below the first line of trees. A tall pine had toppled over and lay facing them. Its roots had torn a hollow space in the ground that was just large enough for two boys.

'It's not quite the Hilton,' Beck said.

'Let's just say there's room for improvement. So, let's improve.' James dropped his bergen on the ground and looked around.

The hollow needed a roof. The fallen tree was a good source of branches, so James got busy removing a few thin ones. They didn't have an axe or a machete so he had to rely on brute strength, working the branches back and forth, teeth gritted, until the wood snapped.

Meanwhile Beck used a flat stone to dig a drainage ditch around the top of their camp. If it rained during the night, water would flow into the ditch and go round them, rather than coming tumbling into the hollow and drenching them.

'Expecting rain?' James asked.

'Probably not. It's still the dry season, just. The monsoon season starts in June, and it won't get this far north until a couple of weeks later, at least. But we're surrounded by mountains, and rain and mountains go together like . . . um . . .'

'Two very togethery things.'

'Exactly. So I'm just making sure.'

Beck had seen one or two monsoons in his time. Damp air swept in from the Indian Ocean and dumped its load on the land. Most of the Indian subcontinent had endless rainy days for a quarter of the year. Life became hot, humid and wet. It was vital to the farmers; it was highly inconvenient to any campers.

While James was attacking the tree, Beck started to gather together sticks and twigs for a fire.

'We've still got the stove,' James pointed out.

'Yeah, but I want to keep the fire going all night. The stove will just run out of gas. This is for heat, not cooking.'

Beck built the small pile in the hollow. First he laid the smallest, driest twigs in a mound the size of both fists clenched together. That was the kindling, the heart of the fire. The bigger sticks were laid on top, looking a bit like the frame of a tepee. Beck struck a match and held it to the kindling. The dry wood, thick with pine resin, started to crackle and spit almost at once. The fire caught quickly. Flame licked its way up the small pile and the air above it began to shimmer with heat.

They took the branches that James had gathered and laid them over the hollow, overlapping to block out any draughts. They left a space in the middle for the wood smoke to escape. Then they sat cross-legged on either side of the fire and chewed on a ration of tahr meat. They didn't talk. James's brief spell of chattiness seemed to be over. Again, Beck could only imagine what thoughts were whirling around his head.

Well, for the time being, they had a camp that was dry, sheltered and warm. Things could be worse. A good night's sleep, some food to eat – they didn't fix everything but they made a lot of things seem more fixable.

The fire was dying down. Once it was smouldering, Beck would fill in the smoke hole in their covering with another couple of bigger and longer branches. Then they would be snug and warm until morning.

He fastened the bergen with the food and pushed himself to his feet. His legs protested – like him, they had been through a lot that day and had been enjoying the rest. 'Just have to hang this in a tree, then we can turn in,' he said.

James turned a puzzled face up at him. 'Eh?'

'Food can attract bears. So you hang it up in branches, away from your camp—'

Beck froze as he heard a mighty roar just metres

away, on the other side of their branch roof. It was behind where James had been sitting. Beck didn't even see his friend move, but somehow James was suddenly standing next to Beck, staring at where the bellow had come from.

Then a powerful pair of claws thrust through the branches – and suddenly half the roof wasn't there any more. A sleek head covered in dark fur lunged towards them. The blunt muzzle opened to reveal powerful jaws lined with teeth that could bite through bone. The creature roared again, with a blast of hot breath that stank of rotting meat.

Beck's precaution about hanging up the food had come too late.

The bear had already found them.

Chapter 13

The bear leaped down into the hollow. The boys didn't even hesitate. They were already scrambling up the other side.

The huge beast trampled on the fire and reared up on its hind legs. It had to be a metre and a half high, its fur dark and sleek, like a black cat's, but with a ragged white V-shaped mark across its chest. Beck's mental database had already classed it as an Asian black bear. Mostly herbivorous but, when the chance came along, carnivorous as well. They were certainly known to attack humans without provocation. Like this one was now doing.

'Shout at it!' Beck yelled. He put his words into action by thrusting his head forward and bellowing with the full force of his lungs. '*R-aa-aa-aa-rh!*'

'*Aaaaah!*' James's scream joined in a split second later.

Some bears, you played dead with. Beck had done that before. A grizzly bear might attack you, but only because it felt threatened or thought you were attacking its cubs. Lie down, don't move, and it got the message that you weren't a danger.

But if a bear was going to attack you for no reason, it wouldn't be fobbed off with a dead body. There was no point running or climbing. The bear could run and climb better. That just left one thing. Make it think that you were just as bad and dangerous.

The bear rumbled and dropped down onto all fours. It didn't take its eyes off Beck.

'*That's right!*' Beck shouted. He banged his fists on his chest. '*And now push off!*'

But instead the bear lunged forward. Beck stepped smartly backwards and his foot caught on a tree root. He tumbled over and the bear lashed out with hooked claws that could have torn him open. He squirmed out of the way and the tips of the claws only caught his leg. It was like someone tearing a red-hot blade through his skin.

And James immediately stopped screaming. 'Hey, Beck, are you all—?'

The bear rounded on him and lurched up onto its hind feet again.

'*Aaaaah!*' It was hard to tell if that was James playing at being big and dangerous, or James screaming in fear. Beck's eyes were watering from the pain, but he saw James step forward, clench his fist and swing a punch at the bear's jaw. The bear gave a surprised grunt and took a step back. It was probably the first time its prey had ever resorted to a right hook.

And then it roared in anger and strode forward again, its front legs raised, claws bared. James had forgotten his brief instant of courage and stood rooted to the spot with wide-eyed terror. He had about one second left to live.

Beck was already on his feet and hobbling forward. The nearest thing that might serve as a weapon was James's bergen – the one with the food, which he had been about to hang in a tree. He raised it up and swung it at the bear's head. '*I said, push off!*'

The bear swung round and its claw snatched

the bergen out of Beck's hands. But immediately its attention was diverted. It gave another grunt, as if to say *Hey, food!* and then flung the bergen down and tore it open, thrusting its head inside.

'Come on,' James gasped. He grabbed Beck's arm and helped him limp away from the camp as fast as he could. Beck had the presence of mind to grab his own bergen and the boys disappeared into the trees, leaving the bear alone with its feast.

Chapter 14

Beck hissed through gritted teeth as James trickled water onto the gash in his leg. 'Don't waste it.'

It was a deep, ragged cut between his thigh and his knee. It was clotting up, but blood still welled slowly out of it. James had given up trying to mop the blood away. Beck thought the best they could do was let it dry naturally.

James's water canister was back at the camp. The canister he was using was only half full. For the time being it was all the water they had.

'We can get more water tomorrow,' James said practically. 'We can't get you a new leg. It's got to be cleaned.'

Beck glumly agreed. Everything on the tip of the bear's claws – rotten meat, dirt, germs – was in the wound and would fester nicely. The thick fabric of his trousers had saved it from being even deeper. Those claws could have cut through to the bone with no trouble, and then he really would have been in trouble. But even a flesh wound could go bad very quickly.

'Anyway,' James added, 'what else could we use?'

Beck forced a grin. His teeth were already bared but he drew his lips back even further. 'Urine's sterile. It's not ideal but it'll wash a wound clean.'

James gave him a cold look. 'First, no way. Second, right now I don't think I could – and third, *no way*!'

Beck wondered if he should introduce James to his friend Peter. Peter had trodden on a sea urchin in Indonesia. Spines had been driven into his foot. The best way to clean the wound had been for Beck to . . .

Maybe not. How would he introduce them? *James, Pete; Pete, James. James tried to kill me once. I peed on Pete's foot*.

He had interesting friends.

They had kept going, up the slope and into the woods, until they could no longer hear the slurp and snuffle of the bear eating their food. They had settled down at the foot of a large rock, their backs against the hard stone. If the bear came for them, it could only come from one direction. James had already found a stout branch to use as a weapon, and gathered together a small pile of stones to hurl.

Beck's bergen had the first aid kit in it, and a few clean clothes, in addition to his water bottle. James used a clean T-shirt to mop Beck's wound and then wrapped the bandage tightly around his leg. Then Beck put his trousers back on, which immediately made him look a lot worse because they were still stained with blood. James made him put the extra T-shirts on too.

'You could go into shock. You need to stay warm.'

One thing James *had* picked up was proper first aid training. Beck couldn't argue. And warmth was going to be an issue. They didn't have a fire and starting one might attract the bear's attention again. It was going to be a long cold night.

'And now sleep. I'll keep watch.'

'You can't stay awake all night,' Beck protested.

'Huh. Watch me.'

'We'll take turns. Hour on, hour off.'

James shrugged. 'OK. But I start. Try to get some sleep.'

Beck eased himself down onto the hard ground. He winced as he stuck his leg out straight. A line of pain ran up it, as if the bear's claws were slicing into it all over again. It throbbed in time with his heartbeat.

Just what I need, he thought as sleep overtook him. This would really slow them down. And a delay against Lumos could be fatal . . .

Chapter 15

Beck prodded the remains of James's bergen with his toe. It had been shredded by claws like steel. It would not be carrying anything else ever again.

His leg still throbbed and he was reluctant to move. He stood still while James scouted around the remains of their camp. Occasionally – about every thirty seconds – he slapped at a midge. Eventually he stopped bothering.

The branches of the roof had been tossed aside. The fire was out. James's water canister had been bitten in two. The stove had been trampled to bits. The box of matches was ground into the earth next to it. Beck pushed it back into shape as best he could. A dozen or so matches were still intact. He slid the box into the zip-lock bag he kept in the side pocket of his bergen.

James came back with everything he could find. 'The tahr's all gone.' He held up a plastic packet in one hand and a crumpled paper bag in the other. 'One packet of noodles, and it didn't think much of the Himalayan candy. And that's all we have.'

Their eyes met.

They had the food in James's hand. They had the clothes they stood in, plus a few spares. They had a length of rope. Everything else was lost, including one member of their party. Compared to what they had set out with, it was a disaster.

But they couldn't go back, and they had the GPS. It had been in Beck's pocket and it was still there.

'We have a direction,' Beck said firmly, 'and a name.'

'Yeah. Sangmu. Who is Sangmu? Or what?' James puffed out his cheeks. 'We could ask, I suppose.'

'*Sangmu? Anyone seen Sangmu?*' Beck shook his head. 'They'd call the police and that would be the end of it.'

'You think the local police work for Lumos?'

'They don't need to. Anyone who came across two lost kids would do the same, anywhere in the world. But, yeah, Lumos would get to hear of it. The one thing we can't do is look lost or attract attention.'

'So we keep heading for the coordinates Ian gave you. And we look out for Sangmu.'

'Sounds like a plan,' Beck concluded.

'Sounds like a *rubbish* plan.'

'But it's the only one we've got.'

'Yeah, I know.' James slid his arms through the straps of the surviving bergen and waved a hand at Beck's leg. 'How is it?'

Beck took a few steps. When he woke up that morning – cold and stiff, because James had insisted on keeping watch all night without disturbing him – his leg had been on fire. It had now died down to a dull glow, or maybe he was just getting used to it. He had tried walking with a stick but it was too slow. If he just threw himself forward, and made his legs work like they usually did, and ignored the pain, then he could keep going at almost a normal walking speed.

'It's fine.'

He could tell that James didn't believe him.

''Kay.' James held up the remaining water canister. He also waved a fly away from his eyes at the same time as Beck slapped at another midge. 'Well, first thing we need to do is fill this up.'

They emerged from the trees and looked up at the sky. Early in the morning birds tended to circle watering holes.

Beck already knew there had to be water nearby. The biggest clue was the flies and midges that were buzzing around. They loved to swarm near water. But birds were easier to spot . . .

And then there was the evidence of their ears. Beck held up a hand and they paused. Then they looked at each other and smiled. The chuckling sound of water running over rocks brushed against their hearing. They started walking again, and after five minutes they came to the river.

The water was cool and clear, fresh from the mountains. It hadn't had time to slow down yet and it ran past them quickly enough to make waves. It was three or four metres across, and Beck wouldn't have wanted to try and cross it.

'Ta-dah!' James looked so pleased you might have thought he had produced it personally. 'And it should be safe to drink, so close to the source. Nothing's had time to make it dirty yet.' He took a step forward to kneel down beside the water.

Beck put out a hand to stop him. 'We don't know there aren't any dead animals upstream.' A rotting animal could be quietly sending poison downstream and they wouldn't know until they got ill.

James squinted up the river. 'How far?'

'Say, five hundred metres? Five minutes' walk.'

'Fine. I'll walk for five minutes and tell you if I see anything. You rest.'

Gratefully, Beck sat down with his leg straight in front of him. James set off at an eager saunter. A hundred metres upstream, the river came round a corner out of a side valley. James went round the corner and disappeared.

Soon afterwards he reappeared and waved. He looked especially pleased with himself as he approached Beck.

'Not a dead animal in sight, and I've got an extra surprise for you.'

'What?' Beck asked cautiously.

James just smiled even more widely and shook his head. 'All in good time, Master Beck!'

Chapter 16

Beck let him play his game. He allowed James to remove the bandage from his leg, and wash the wound – now clotting nicely – with fresh water, and put a new bandage on.

He looked moodily down the valley. They didn't know where they were and only had a vague idea of where they were going. How far could they travel that day? He didn't know that either.

'We need to get breakfast,' he said. 'We need to stock up on energy.'

'Breakfast is part of the surprise.' James tied the bandage in place with a final tug and stood up again. 'You rest here.' He gave Beck an extra big smile. 'Hey, why the long face? Cheer up. You'll enjoy the surprise. And look. You're always going on about nature – well, there's a fantastic rainbow.' He waved a hand in the general direction of the horizon, and set off while Beck was looking.

True, it wasn't a bad rainbow, Beck thought. It was many miles away and it arced up above the level of the mountains. Despite the distance he could clearly pick out the vibrant bands of colour.

The day was warming up. The sound of running water was soothing. Beck felt he could very easily just lie down here and doze. It would do his leg good.

Unfortunately dozing was what he couldn't afford to do. They had to move on. Lumos wasn't going to come to them. What was keeping James?

He looked at his watch, and was surprised to see that it was getting on for half an hour since James had left. If this surprise meant just sitting around and waiting for something to happen, then it wasn't worth it. And if James had gone and fallen into the river or over a cliff or . . .

Beck muttered under his breath and pushed himself to his feet. His leg had seized up again and he had to force it into motion. As before, once he had got his body into a rhythm, then it was almost like walking normally.

He followed the route James had taken. The banks were lined with thick rhododendron bushes. The air was scented with their pollen. There was no sign of James, but that wasn't surprising because he couldn't see more than a few metres ahead. The river continued to curve, and Beck was walking along a narrow strip of ground between the water and clumps of flowers taller than his head.

Then Beck paused, and sniffed. He could smell smoke. Wood smoke, strong enough to block out the smell of the flowers. For some reason it just added to his unease.

There was a sudden loud buzz in his ear, and a moment later he felt something settle on his hand. He was about to brush it away – and then his hand froze, just a couple of centimetres away from a painful sting.

One of the largest bees he had ever seen sat on the back of his wrist. He recognized it as a Himalayan honey bee, the largest bee in the world. It was a good three centimetres long, with a brown-gold body and wings. It crawled over his skin for a moment and he felt the tickle as it probed for pollen. Eventually it decided that Beck wasn't some unusual flower and took off again.

The drone of its wings didn't die away. It blended into a hum that had been there in the background for some time without Beck realizing it. A hum caused by many hundreds, perhaps thousands of bees . . .

The sense of foreboding grew stronger and Beck hurried forward.

He came out onto a stretch of flat rocky ground where the bushes stopped. The river ran along one side. On the far side was a low cliff. James stood with his back to Beck, craning his neck up at something on the rock face. Next to him a pile of burning rhododendron branches belched out a column of thick grey smoke.

And in between, the air was thick with angry bees, growing angrier by the minute.

Chapter 17

Bees flew past Beck's head like buzzing bullets. He forced himself not to flinch. Bee vision was based on movement. If you stood still, they assumed you were part of the landscape.

James didn't seem to have noticed the bees or Beck. He was still staring intently at something above his head. Beck followed the line of his gaze, and his heart thudded. Halfway up the rock there was an overhang, and below it hung a golden mass twice the size of a human head. Its surface was crawling with more bees. It was a bees' nest. It was made of slabs of gooey honeycomb, glued onto the rock and dripping with natural honey. It was big enough to house several thousand bees, and James had managed to upset them all.

Beck took a breath, intending to shout, *James! What the heck are you doing!* – and then he let it out very gently. Bees also homed in on carbon dioxide in exhaled breath.

Unfortunately he couldn't stop breathing altogether, so he just spoke quietly, making the question calm and mild. 'James . . . ?'

'Oh, hi, Beck.' James turned round casually and recoiled as he saw the swarm for the first time. 'Whoa! Where did they come from?'

'Uh – from the nest?'

'Oh. Yeah. I was reading about Nepalese bee hunters. They use smoke to calm the bees down. Don't worry – they recover once the smoke's gone. But they calm right down, and then you can get at the honey safely.' The first shadow of doubt began to creep over his face. 'Uh . . . They don't look that calm, do they? Maybe I haven't used enough smoke. Hang on.'

He threw another branch onto the pile. The buzzing of the bees was now a vibration that seemed to go through Beck's body. He could swear it had just gone up a notch. Any moment now they would stop faffing about and go on the offensive. The poison from that number of stings, all at once, could send him and James into toxic shock. They would die, slowly and painfully.

'James,' he said, more urgently. He itched to run forward but he was still trying not to attract attention. 'Just come away from the fire . . .'

'It's OK! This was going to be my surprise. Honey! It's sweet and full of energy and it's also a natural antiseptic for your leg. Haven't you ever done this?'

'Please, just back away. Slowly. Don't make sudden movements . . .'

James waved him down. 'It's OK. I think it's safe.' To Beck's horror he reached up above him to the nearest piece of honeycomb and snapped it off.

'*Ow!*' James dropped the honeycomb and stared at his hand. His face was twisted with pain. '*Jeez*, that hurts!' He glared up at the comb, as if angry that the bees hadn't read the same website as he had. 'That wasn't meant to—' He slapped at his neck. '*Ow!*'

The bees had identified the threat and they were gathering, growing thicker in the air around him.

'Just run!' Beck shouted. It was too late to worry

about attracting or angering the bees. James just needed to get away from there. But James stood there, frozen to the spot with fear, as he finally understood the danger he was in. He was only half visible through the cloud of insects.

There was nothing for it. Beck forced his aching leg to obey him and broke into a stumbling run.

James was flailing with his arms to wave the bees away, which just enraged them further. He had obviously given up on the whole honey plan. Unfortunately he was panicking now, which wasn't helping at all. It was as if the panic had frozen his rational senses.

Beck ducked under his waving arms, grabbed him and forced him towards the river.

'*Ow!* Hey, where—?'

'*Move!*'

The buzzing grew louder. Beck and James stumbled towards the water, locked together in Beck's firm grip. Insect bodies scraped against Beck's face. He squeezed his eyes almost shut – he squinted to see where they were going. He had vivid images of the creatures tangling in his hair, or crawling down his neck and up his sleeves.

Surely they had to be almost there! The clouds of bees were so thick that Beck could barely see where they were going. Were they even heading the right way? Had they somehow missed the river? Were they heading back towards the nest?

They stumbled over the edge of the bank and toppled headfirst into the freezing cold water. The river closed over their heads.

Beck had been expecting the jolt to the system. A shock like that made you just want to gasp. He forced his mouth to stay shut. James spluttered and took in a bellyful of water. He immediately began to convulse and choke, fighting his way to the surface.

The current was too strong to fight against and it whisked them away. At first Beck tried to help James, but then he let him go. Holding on would just drown them both. They struggled to keep their heads above the surface. Water splashed over their faces and the cold almost paralysed their lungs, as if iron bands were wrapped around them.

A bee flew in front of Beck's eyes and he ducked his head down, but he needn't have worried. The swarm was now far behind them, and the two boys were facing an even bigger problem.

Beck parted chattering teeth to suggest that they should make for the shore again, when the current suddenly grew stronger. A wave washed over his head and he felt a new force take hold of his body. The river had abruptly changed direction and now ran between narrow rocky banks. There was no way they could swim against this force.

James was trying to face forward, but the weight of his bergen kept pulling him over. All their remaining supplies were in it – they had to keep hold of it.

Beck shouted at him: 'Get your pack off and hold it like a flotation device in front of you. Then just try and float on your back – *phlub*' – a wave filled his mouth and nose – 'feet first, in case you hit something. I'll try and guide you . . .'

And so the current swept them on. Beck did his best to keep them in the main flow of the river – the tongue of the rapids, as it was called. The water was smoothest there and they were clear of the jagged rocks. The moment they were through the rapids, Beck started to steer them towards the shore. The cold was leaching the heat out of their bodies. They had already been in the river for several minutes, and in water this cold they had about ten minutes max before hypothermia set in.

They had emerged into a narrow river valley. There were trees on either side and a gravel shore between those and the water. Their feet touched the bottom and they could now stand up, staggering against the force that still pulled at their legs. Finally they dropped onto the bank, dripping and shivering.

Cold, Beck thought grimly. *Cold, wet, and well and truly lost. This is starting to get interesting*.

Chapter 18

James hauled his bergen up the bank and sat hugging his knees. He looked as if he was about to burst into tears.

'That wasn't meant to happen— *Ow!*' His hand went to his neck.

Beck looked around quickly – had the bees caught up with them?

But no. Looking closer, he saw the red spot on James's skin, and the black speck in the middle. The bee had left its stinger in him. It was barbed, so it wouldn't just fall out, and there was a small sac of venom at the end.

Beck quickly grabbed James's hand before he could touch the sting. 'Careful. You could just end up squeezing more poison in.'

James gritted his teeth and shivered. Beck couldn't tell if it was with pain, or cold from their drenching, or both.

'Can you get it out?'

Beck peered at it. 'Have you got your knife?'

'Sure . . .' James felt at his side for his belt. Then he felt on the other side. His face fell even further. 'It must have come off in the river.'

'OK. Basically we need to scrape it out with something hard and flat.' Beck studied his fingers. Human fingertips were the worst for this. They were too blunt and stubby and would squash the venom sac. Fingernails, on the other hand, were fine. He was glad he didn't bite his.

'No offence,' he said as he got to work, 'but that was really, really stupid. You know we could have been killed?'

He put his little finger next to the sting and slid the fingernail under the venom sac. It took a couple of tries, but eventually the sting came out, venom sac and all. Beck flicked it away. 'So please, please check with me first? Anything involving animals or . . . well, basically, anything!'

'If it has more than two legs, or wings, it's Beck's department,' James promised. 'Fine by me.'

Beck checked where the sting had been. A red mark surrounded the tiny puncture, but he had got everything out. 'We need to wash this . . .'

'Right.' James snorted, still shivering. 'Because what I could really do with right now is more water.'

Beck tugged the bergen open and pulled out a drenched but clean T-shirt. He used it to dab at James's neck. 'Running water washes away dirt and germs.' He sat back and surveyed his work critically. 'You'll be OK. I'd like to put a cold compress on that to take down the swelling, but . . .'

'What would work?'

'Oh . . .' Beck had to grin at the ludicrous idea. 'Coconut meat is a good one.'

'Great. Coconuts.'

'Or mix mud and ashes together . . .'

'Plenty of mud,' James said, looking around.

'You need the ashes too. For sterilizing. Otherwise you're just putting dirt back into it.'

'I don't think we'll be making fires anytime soon.' James shrugged. 'I can bear it.' He jumped to his feet and held out a hand to help Beck up. Suddenly he gave an abrupt laugh. 'I know where we could get coconuts, though. There's this island . . .'

Beck had to grin as he clambered up. 'This island' was where he and James – and James's mother – had been washed up after Abby had managed to sink the ship they were on. Like so many Lumos plans, that wasn't quite what was meant to happen. It seemed to run in the family . . .

Suddenly Beck's head felt very light. He stumbled forward, and James had to catch him.

'Hey, you OK? You looked like you almost passed out.'

'Just . . .' Beck looked down at his injured leg. 'Everything.'

'OK. Well, you sit down and rest, OK? And we need to get out of these wet things or we'll just get hypothermia. Right?'

Beck nodded wearily. His thoughts were dazed. Hypothermia could strike quickly – like, if you were submerged in ice-cold water – or it could just creep up on you – like, if you stayed in wet clothes. It was your body's way of conserving heat. It took warmth from the extremities first – the hands and feet. But if you didn't take care, pretty soon your whole body would start shutting down. Your mind got confused and ultimately your vital organs would pack up.

James shook Beck back to reality. He found Beck a sheltered spot to lie down, out of the wind and facing the sun. He stripped Beck down to his base layer of clothes and spread the garments out to dry on a piece of rock. James, also in his shorts, laid everything else from the bergen out in the sun. *Sunbathing in Nepal*, Beck thought drowsily. *Not what I ever expected to be doing . . .*

He sat up abruptly. No, stuff this. He wasn't going to get stronger by sunning himself. He wasn't a plant.

What he needed – what they both needed – was protein.

He got up, put on his boots, leaving his socks to dry, and limped towards the river.

James looked up in surprise. 'Where are you going?'

'I'm going to find food,' Beck said firmly. 'We mustn't get lazy.'

Chapter 19

Beck headed a little further downstream, where the river turned away from him. The outside bend of a river always tended to be shallower as grit piled up there. The current was also more gentle. Fish often rested there, in slower water.

The water was clear and Beck could easily see the rocky bed. The first thing he looked for was a pool where fish might have saved him the bother and trapped themselves. There was no point in making life harder than it had to be.

But no – no pools. He was going to have to work a bit harder.

A metre from the bank a pair of stones stood clear of the water, about half a metre apart. Beck waded out to inspect the two rocks, wincing as the icy water rose up to his knees. The water ran quickly between them like a miniature version of the small canyon he and James had come through earlier. Perfect – that was the start of the trap.

Over the next half-hour Beck worked slowly and carefully in the shallows. The whole point of this was to catch a fish, preferably more than one. The fish was for eating, to restore his strength. There was no point in burning more calories than he was going to get back.

Downstream of the two rocks he built a small corral out of stones, to catch anything that went through the gap between them. He lugged the stones there one at a time. Each was big enough for his needs, small enough that he didn't wear himself out. Eventually he had a small semicircular enclosure. The stones were rough and didn't fit together perfectly, so he plugged as many gaps as he could with smaller rocks and gravel. It didn't matter that water could still get through the smaller holes. All that mattered was that fish couldn't.

Next, on the upstream side of the rocks, Beck built two miniature walls that reached out from the gap. One went from the gap to the bank, blocking off that route for any fish that came this way. The other went as far out into the river as he could get, before the current grew too strong and the water too deep. He liked to think of these walls reaching out from the entrance like a warm, friendly embrace.

Last of all, he closed the gap up a little. He took a pair of stones and positioned them on either side, to reduce the width of the entrance by about a half. It had the added advantage of speeding up the water that flowed between them. Fish would swim into the trap but they would be disinclined to turn and swim out again against that current. They wouldn't realize that they had strayed into a little rocky pool with no other way out. Fish were easily pleased. They could happily just coast about in their little space thinking secret fishy thoughts. Hopefully the last of those thoughts would be: *Hey, why am I suddenly leaving the water?*

Beck's hands and feet were numb with cold, but the rest of him was comfortably warm from the exercise. He sat on one of the big stones and gratefully let the warmth reach his extremities. He could sit here and wait. Or he could speed up the process a little.

'Hey, James!'

James had managed to get a small fire going, with sticks and one of the matches they had water-proofed. He looked up suspiciously. 'What?'

'Want to throw some stones together?'

James stood up, puzzled. 'Eh?'

'I've made a fish trap, but I need you to drive the fish down towards it. Just keep throwing stones to make a splash!'

James started to walk along the bank, tossing stones into the water. He soon got into his stride and was soon pelting the water with them, as if venting all his pain and loss and anger on the river.

Meanwhile Beck crouched on one of the rocks at the entrance to the trap and waited.

And there it was! His first customer of the day. A flickering shadow beneath the surface. Slowly Beck slid his hand into the water . . .

Chapter 20

James came running down the bank. 'Any luck?'

'Uh-huh . . .'

Beck kept his eyes on the fish. He could feel the water taking the warmth out of his hand again. His fingers felt like they were slowly turning to ice. That was good. Fish were very sensitive to temperature. His hand was cooling down to the same temperature as the water . . .

Slowly his hand and the fish moved closer to each other. The fish didn't seem unduly worried, though it could have shot away with one flick of its fins. Its body was sleek and streamlined, about thirty or forty centimetres long. Beck guessed it was probably a species of trout, which made it all the better.

He slowly wiggled his fingers and slid his hand under the fish's belly, imitating the flow of water. Then, before the fish could react, he curled his fingers and scooped it out. The fish flew through the air, wriggling, and landed on the bank. Its silver scales glistened and flashed in the sun as it twisted and writhed around. Beck leaped after it before it could flop its way back into the water again, though his injured leg protested. With one hand he dug his fingers into the gills, the only place to get a grip on its scaly body. He grabbed the tail with the other hand so that its body was curved, and sank his teeth into its spine just behind its head.

Cold, fresh juices spurted into his mouth – water and blood and the natural oils of the fish, all mingled together. The flesh was firm, just chewy enough to make it worth biting.

This was better than instant noodles! He could feel the fish scales and blood covering his face but he didn't care. He chewed his way down one side of the fish's muscular flanks, stripping away the flesh but leaving the guts, which would just taste foul.

James was staring at him, slightly pale. 'Um . . . uck?' he murmured.

Beck grinned and James flinched. Beck quickly closed his mouth again and wiped his teeth with his tongue.

'The other half is yours,' he mumbled between chews. He laid the fish down on a stone and moved a little way along the bank, well away from the trap, to splash water on his face. Being downstream, none of this would fall into the water and scare other fish away from the entrance.

'Come and have a go!' Beck called. 'You'll pick it up easily if you take your time.'

James was a quick learner and only lost one fish: at first, rather than flinging it onto the bank, as Beck had done, he had tried to hold onto it. It slithered and wriggled in his hands as he danced about on one of the rocks and tried to keep a grip.

'*Whoa . . . whoa . . . oh-h-h . . . !*' With a loud splash, both James and the fish were back in the river.

The second one he managed to land on the bank. He grabbed it and held it up triumphantly, though it wriggled hard to escape. His thumb and forefinger

113

were dug into its gills to stop it getting away.

'And now you bite it,' Beck said. 'Make sure you bite through the spine. That'll kill it at once.'

James pulled a face. 'I didn't go to all that trouble to eat sushi, thanks. I'll take my fish cooked.'

'Your choice.' And with that, Beck picked up his half-eaten fish and carried on munching. Blood, flesh and scales refuelled his tired and injured body.

Chapter 21

Beck felt a lot better with a good-sized fish inside him – even one eaten raw. He had to admit that the smell of James's fish cooking on the end of a stick was also pretty good. Maybe he should catch another . . . No, no need. Beck always knew when enough was enough. You caught and ate what you needed – that was all. There would be plenty of chances later to cook food.

By now everything was dry again and they could get their trousers and shirts back on.

James insisted on checking Beck's leg wound one more time. 'How does it feel?'

'Meh.' Beck shrugged. Truth to tell, it still throbbed in time with his heart. That wasn't going to go away. The gash from the bear's claw had clotted over so there was no more blood, but the skin around it was still red and raw.

In short, it was far from perfect, but it was as good as it was going to get.

'Just wrap it up again,' he said. 'It'll be fine.'

James looked doubtful, but he unfurled a fresh strip of bandage and tied it in place. Beck filled up the water canister and they packed their few possessions into the bergen, which James insisted on carrying. Beck didn't like to feel he was being nursemaided, but he was glad he didn't have any more weight for his leg to carry.

'So.' James looked at him expectantly. 'Which way?'

Beck checked the GPS. Its waterproof casing had kept the water out, but he looked at the power bar on the screen. It was still green, but it wouldn't be long before it reached orange. Once before, Beck had been stuck in the wilderness with a dead GPS, miles from the nearest recharging point. From now on he would only turn it on from time to time, just to check their course.

He slowly rotated until he and the GPS were

facing roughly north-west, towards the side of the valley. 'Thataway.'

'How far do we have to go?'

'We could walk it in a day – if we could walk in a straight line.' Beck squinted up at the way ahead. 'Problem is . . .'

'I know. Mountains.'

You simply couldn't walk in a straight line through mountains. You went over, or round, and sometimes you annoyingly had to backtrack to avoid a dead end. But unless someone had kindly dug a tunnel for you, you did not walk in a straight line.

Beck flicked the GPS off again and pointed. 'That peak there? That's our next landmark. I'll check our course again when we get there.'

They set off, away from the river, heading slowly upwards. Once again, Beck gritted his teeth and forced his legs into a deliberate walking rhythm, ignoring the pain that seemed to jab into his bones with each stride. The sounds of running water faded away behind them, replaced by boots snapping wood and crunching through pine needles as they pushed into the trees that lined the valley. And then there was a loud groan from both of them as they came out of the trees and found themselves facing a sheer wall of rock.

It hadn't been obvious from down by the river, with the trees in the way. Beck had hoped the valley just kept sloping upwards until they were up at the top. But no: the ground suddenly lurched up vertically. If they could get up on top of this, maybe they could keep walking as planned. But that was a big 'if'.

They craned their heads back to look up at the top.

'Thirty metres?' James asked.

'More like forty.'

'We could do it. We've got a rope.'

'Yeah, about fifteen metres . . .'

Once upon a time – and it now seemed a long time ago, though it was less than twenty-four hours – Beck would have loved the challenge of climbing this rock face. With a decent rope, and all the right climbing gear, and an experienced colleague – and, oh yes, a leg that hadn't been torn open by a bear.

'It's just too risky,' he said reluctantly. 'We'll follow

the valley north and hope there's another way up further along.' He looked thoughtfully at the trees. There was a narrow strip between the trunks and the base of the cliff, and they could probably walk along that. But you never knew when it might suddenly vanish and they could find themselves fighting their way through undergrowth. There was no point in making life more difficult than it had to be.

'Back to the river,' he said with a sigh. 'At least the banks are clear.'

Chapter 22

They turned and set off back down the slope – at a slight angle so as to meet the river further along from their campsite.

'Could we build a raft?' James said hopefully as they reached the bank and turned north. The ground here was mostly flat. Tough, scrubby grass jostled for space with small rocks.

Beck stumbled over a hidden stone and his injured leg gave an extra jab as all his weight came down in it – enough to make him hiss through his teeth. At that precise moment, the prospect of travelling by raft was mighty tempting. He remembered the *Ptarmigan*, the raft he and Tikaani had built in Alaska, where it had been the best and quickest way of getting along. Here it was different.

'We don't know what's ahead,' he said reluctantly. 'Rafts are good for slow rivers, but we know how quickly this river changes – there could be rapids or waterfalls or hidden rocks. It could be smashed to pieces and we'd just get soaked and frozen again. Plus it would take some time to build it in the first place, and we don't really have the material . . .'

James coughed and looked at all the trees.

'Nothing big enough lying around, and no axe to cut anything down,' Beck corrected himself. 'So . . . no. We keep walking.'

'We keep walking,' James said with a sigh.

They followed the river downstream, heading north. Beck was pleased to find that his decision to walk had been a good one. The valley had never been very wide, and now it grew narrower as it wound its way into the distance. As a result, the river speeded up. It flowed along briskly, as if too impatient to pause to make conversation. White, thrashing water and waves spoke of hidden obstacles below. They would have had a hard time on a raft.

But walking along the river wasn't easy either. The bank was the only really clear and flat stretch of ground, but it wasn't always smooth. It was eaten into by streams that came down from the hills, or chunks taken out by erosion. This close to the water, the ground often became boggy or was blocked by huge boulders, so the boys had to keep navigating their way round obstacles.

The sides of the valley were steep and rocky. There was a thin line of trees further up, but no larger plants between them and the water. And that only meant one thing: the river often flooded and swept anything else away. Fortunately, there was no sign of it doing that at the moment. But there was no footpath, no beaten track – a sure sign that not many people came this way.

And it was Mosquito City Central. The little creatures were drawn by the moisture in the heavy, humid air and they hummed past Beck's ears with a sound like a tiny electric saw. They flew into his hair and made it itch like crazy. Their bites were sharp jabs in his skin; they slowly swelled up, big and red and juicy.

James suffered just as much. It was quite entertaining listening to him as they trudged along.

'Ow!' – *slap* – 'Ow!' – *slap* . . .

Beck had resolved to ignore them as much as he could and let them feast upon his blood. He and James were just two boys, and the total mosquito population of Nepal was probably several billion. He knew when they were outnumbered.

They walked in single file with Beck in the lead. And then, suddenly, hearing James's shout of surprise and fright, followed by the hiss of an angry animal, Beck whirled round.

Chapter 23

James was rooted to the spot. An animal the size of a large cat sat on top of a boulder. It stared hard at them out of two round, pebble-like eyes. Beck took a step forward and it immediately reared up on its hind legs, hissing from a mouth lined with needle-sharp teeth.

The creature's hair was thick and gingery, like a cross between a fox and a bear. It had four stubby, powerful legs, a shaggy striped tail as long as its body, white nose and pointed ears, and a white mask around its eyes.

All in all it was like someone had mixed a bear, a panda and a fox together, and boiled it down to house-cat size.

'It was curled up under that rock . . .' James paused. 'What the heck is it?'

Beck had to bite back a laugh. 'It's a red panda. They're rare but there's enough of them, away from humans.'

'A *panda*?' James said in disbelief.

'It's only distantly related to the black-and-white kind. They're not fierce – well, not if they don't get upset. C'mon, let's keep going.'

'OK . . .' James gave the red panda a wide berth as he circled round its rock.

It eyed him suspiciously in return. Like a cat, it kept its eyes on them as they walked away, poised to make a break for it if they suddenly decided to come back.

Then everything was back to normal.

'Ow' – *slap* – 'I *hate* these mosquitoes! Is it just me or are they getting worse?'

'I know. I hate them too. We'll get used to them though.'

Sometimes Beck wondered whether James and the great outdoors were made for each other. Then he would remember that James had spent a couple of months living alone on a desert island. He had survived, and he had done it the hard way.

That was the point when he had resolved to turn his back on Lumos. The hardship and the wild had changed him.

'I'll never get used to them' – *slap* – 'and we've lost all our repellent. This is going to be a lo-n-n-g walk.'

'Yeah. It is.'

Beck stopped with his hands on his hips and looked down the valley, frowning. Its rocky slopes twisted and turned before they disappeared into the haze. There was no obvious sign of a way out – not in the direction they were heading. Would they ever get out of this stupid place?

And – Beck had to admit it – James was actually right. The mosquitoes hadn't been this bad twenty-four hours earlier.

He cocked an eye up at the trees above them, and slowly broke into a smile. 'OK, I can't get us out of here but I can do something . . .' He started up the slope.

'You know, you're definitely limping,' James commented as they reached the trees.

Beck waved it away – though James was right

(again). His leg really was throbbing. He could feel it swelling against the bandage. He knew that if he looked, the wound would be angry and red. No doubt some infection had got in. Unfortunately there was nothing to be done about that.

The trees were evergreen pines, like Christmas trees on steroids. The piney smell was strong in the air and the ground was a thick carpet of brown, dead needles. Beck wrapped his fingers around the nearest branch and pulled. A handful of fresh needles accumulated in his palm. Like the thick and scaly wood beneath them, they were sticky with resin. He repeated the trick on another branch.

'Get as many as you can hold,' he said. 'Then crush 'em' – he ground his palms together, mashing the needles into a pulp that clung to his skin like glue – 'and do this.'

He rubbed his palms over his face, over the back of his neck, behind his ears and up his bare arms.

'It's natural mosquito repellent. You smell like a furniture store but it keeps them away.'

'Now you're talking!' James eagerly followed suit.

'We'll have to do this every hour.' Beck studied the tree more closely, checking out the pine cones. They looked like little wooden hand grenades, sealed tight against the air and any marauding elements, such as hungry fourteen-year-old boys. He began to search the ground for one that had fallen recently; one where the chips had opened up but the seeds hadn't yet fallen out. He picked up a likely candidate and tapped it into his hand. Up close you could see the wonder of its design. Layer upon layer of curved wooden blocks arranged in spirals, as if a master carpenter had designed them. Each one sheltered a seed. With each tap, some seeds dropped into his hand.

'Pines are great,' he said conversationally. 'You can eat the seeds.' He matched actions to words and tipped the little pile into his mouth. They crunched between his teeth. 'You can eat the inner bark raw. You can brew the needles into a tea. They're both full of vitamins. The sap makes a great glue if you heat it. Or you can even use it as an emergency tooth filling. Cool, eh?'

'Like nature's pharmacy . . .' James said as he

picked up a cone of his own and began to follow Beck's example.

They didn't hang around. The main point of this had been to get the natural repellent on their skin. Then they set off again in a much more positive frame of mind. There were plenty more pines around for them to leave the bark-eating and tea-brewing for later.

They made their way back down to the river. It was still the easiest way along the valley. The resin seemed to do the trick. Mosquitoes buzzed past their ears and hung around in small clouds, but they mostly parted to let the boys through.

The valley grew narrow again. No more trees for the time being, just steep rock faces to their left and right. The sounds of the running water and their boots on rock were clear in the still air. Every noise was magnified back by the stone walls on either side.

That included the sudden high-pitched '*Eek!*' from James.

Beck looked round and frowned. 'What?'

James looked abashed and pointed between two rocks. 'Spider.'

'*Spider?*' Beck said in disbelief. He had once seen James happily pick up a thirty-centimetre-long centipede – shortly before it bit him, of course. He hadn't expected him to react like this to creepy crawlies.

'I was about to walk that way. The web would have gone in my face – that's all.'

Beck grinned and peered closely at the web. It was beautifully made. The strands were short and tight, as if the spider had taken a winch and wound each one up to maximum tautness. The spider itself sat in the middle with its legs wrapped around itself. It was big – maybe the size of a golf ball – but he didn't think it was dangerous.

'Yeah, well, she wouldn't have minded. Look at her, just watching nature go by . . .'

Beck's own words seemed to come back to him from a distance, like someone was repeating them. Repeating them as a lesson: things to look out for . . .

'Oh, crud. . .' he murmured. He looked up and back the way they had come. The sky was dark and overcast.

He could have kicked himself. For a moment he thought of asking James to do the kicking for him. He deserved it. How many signs had he missed?

That fantastic rainbow James had pointed out earlier.

The swarming mosquitoes.

He breathed in through his nose, savouring what he could smell. An extra-strong scent from the trees, as nature opened itself up, ready to receive what was coming.

All things that happened in the couple of hours before a storm.

'There's rain coming,' he said.

Beck quickly glanced up and down the valley. Where they stood, there were no trees and very few plants. And he knew why. Nothing grew very big when the river was constantly washing it away.

'And when it does, this place is going to fill up. We need to get out of here. Now.'

Chapter 24

The first drops began to fall even as he spoke. Swollen, heavy, warm. *The full monsoon*, Beck thought with a sinking feeling.

It wasn't just going to rain, it was going to rain *a lot*. And it had already started, further south. Those dark clouds would already have been dumping their load into the river for hours, and it was all going to come downstream at *them*.

'Make for the high ground.' He matched actions to words by turning away from the river and walking as fast as his injured leg would allow.

James strolled casually beside him. 'It won't fill up that quickly, will it?'

'Yes,' Beck said through teeth that were clamped together against the pain in his thigh. He kept walking.

'It will. I've seen flash floods that were like walls of water five metres high and they just come at you. Or, sure, they can just build up slowly . . . But have you ever seen one of those videos of a town being flooded and cars being swept away?'

'Sure.'

'How high do you think water has to get to do that?'

'Mmm . . . dunno. A couple of metres?'

Beck shook his head. 'Half a metre of fast-moving water will shift a car. And that's why humans who want to stay alive stay out of the way of fast-moving water.'

James glanced back the way they had come. 'Well, no walls of water yet— Oh.'

'What?'

'That rock where the spider was . . .'

'Yes?'

'It's underwater.'

Beck looked back. James was right. The rock, and the flat stretch of bank where they had been walking, was already submerged under fast, frothing water. It was simply unstoppable; nothing got in its way. It would spread out until it could spread no more – which meant until it reached the rock walls on either side of the valley. And then it would just keep rising, leaving them with nowhere to go.

The rain struck with full force. There was no time to stop and put on cagoules, and after about thirty seconds the two boys were drenched through. Beck blinked and wiped water off his face. His longer-than-usual hair hung dripping in front of his eyes and he slicked it back to clear his vision. They couldn't see more than twenty or thirty metres along the valley. Everything just dissolved into the grey blur of the downpour.

A cliff loomed out of the rain ahead of them. They were at the top of the valley slope. Beck could hear the river behind them – the sound of the rain hitting the surface, and the water racing over the rocks. He tried not to think that it sounded like an animal coming after them . . .

Chapter 25

Beck tilted his head back to look up the cliff. Warm rain splashed into his face. It blurred his vision and he couldn't see how high the cliff might be. He was prepared to bet it was a good hundred metres or more.

Something red shot past in the corner of his vision. A red panda – maybe the one they had seen earlier. It reached the cliff and ran up it without a pause. It moved like a cross between a cat and a monkey.

'He's got the right idea. We've got to climb— *Aargh!*' Beck had put all his weight on his bad leg as he tried to lever himself up.

James caught him as he toppled. 'You can't climb if that's going to keep happening!'

'Got to,' Beck muttered. This time he used his good leg to push himself up off the ground. Then he brought his bad leg up beside it. Then his good leg again . . .

And so they climbed. Beck just had to go up one step at a time, never relying on his bad leg to hold his weight.

James swarmed easily up alongside him, with four gangly and perfectly healthy limbs. He reminded Beck of a spider, with half the number of legs. Beck remembered James's fear as they climbed out over the abyss that had claimed Ian's life. Maybe he was getting used to heights now, he thought, impressed by his friend's resilience.

'Remember, keep—'

'Keep three points of contact – only move one – got it.' James casually repeated the climbing advice Beck had given him the day before. He seemed to have learned the lesson well.

Beck looked down and saw that the valley had disappeared. The cliff went straight down into water that surged beneath him. He looked away and kept climbing.

'*Whoa!*' James's foot shot out from beneath him. He lurched forward and his face hit the rock. It was the only way he could stop himself from tumbling off altogether.

'Ow.' James's lip had split. He probed it gingerly with his tongue. 'The rock's slippery.'

The rock was more than slippery. It was as wet as they were. Small streams of water ran down it. With every hand- or foothold, they had to take twice as much care.

Beck had no idea how high they had got. James was now slightly ahead of him. He took one last look down: he was pretty sure the water was closer. He wasn't going to look down again.

James stopped. 'Can't go any higher,' he called back down.

'You have to,' Beck shouted back. Even his good leg and his arms were throbbing with the exertion. Clinging to the rock, soaked and chilled by the rain, his fingers felt as limp as overcooked spaghetti. But they had to go on.

'No, I mean, we can't . . . it's just smooth. I wouldn't want to do this even if we had proper equipment.'

Beck came up alongside James and felt his hopes plummet. James was right. Up until now the cliff had offered handy nooks and crannies for fingers and toes. It had been steep, but manageable. Here, Beck suspected a chunk of rock must have split away, years or maybe centuries before. It had left a clean, smooth sheet of stone in its place. They couldn't climb it – plain and simple.

'So . . .' James said, without much hope. 'We could just stay here and hope it doesn't come this high?' He looked dubiously down at the water.

Beck tried to imagine clinging to the rock, shivering and wet, as the strength and energy drained out of them, for the hours it would take for the flood to drain away. They would fall off first.

'Or we go sideways,' he said roughly. 'Find our way past it . . .'

He angled his head out past James to see if there was a way along the cliff in that direction. And then he blinked in surprise. A red, furry face with dark eyes set in a white mask gazed back at him from a few metres away. It took one look at him and abruptly withdrew.

'There's that red panda!'

'Probably come to gloat,' James muttered.

Beck nudged him. 'Just climb along. There must be a cave there. They probably use it for shelter.'

'They've got teeth,' James reminded him as he started to shuffle along the rock face. 'And claws.'

'Yeah, well, I can do a really good roaring sound, remember?'

'Oh, yeah.' James sounded pleased. 'Me too.'

'Yeah, but yours was all girly.'

'Yeah, right! Hey, look, there *is* a cave. Uh . . . hi, pandas?'

The cave was a deep indentation in the rock. A strong animal smell drifted out of it. It went back about three metres and was less than a metre high, but James could swing himself into it and sit bent double. A small family of red pandas crouched at the other end. One of them hissed at him.

'Just ignore it,' Beck shouted. The panda went quiet as James helped him into the cave.

Worn out and drenched, the boys slumped down on the rocky floor and looked out at the rain. The rain that was no longer falling on them. Just that thought on its own made them feel warmer.

'Think the waters have stopped?' James asked.

Beck jerked a thumb towards the back of the cave. 'They obviously do, and they've been around longer. They must be used to this.'

There was no chance of a fire – even if they'd had the wherewithal, Beck wouldn't have made one for the sake of their fellow cave mates.

And so, cold and wet, and in the company of some very wary-looking red pandas, the two boys waited for the storm to pass.

Chapter 26

The rain lasted for another hour. They passed the time by soaking some instant noodles in a cup of water and eating them cold. After that, they could only wait.

Beck sat in the cave entrance and watched the rain slowly clear. James clasped his arms around his knees, hugging himself, gazing gloomily at nothing. The red pandas watched sullenly from the back of the cave, waiting for the two big hairless apes to get out of their home.

Even when the rain stopped, the air was still full of moisture. Somewhere above the clouds, the tropical sun was beating down and turning the rain below into a steam bath. By mid-afternoon the waters had receded and the pair could think about climbing down again.

Beck peered over the edge. 'Hasn't got any less steep.'

James stirred. Beck noted the effort he had to make to get moving, and suddenly realized what had happened. He had allowed James to slide down into depression, and had done nothing about it. *Idiot!* he told himself furiously.

Ian's death still hung in the air. Beck had left James sitting there for an hour with nothing to do but think about it. He had to get James moving – not just physically, but mentally as well. A good mental attitude was just as important to survival as a healthy body.

James looked down the cliff. 'Well, we climbed up,' he said dully.

'Yeah, we did,' Beck agreed. And the effort had been enough to make his leg shriek with pain. He really wasn't confident about being able to climb down again. 'We'll have to use the rope.'

James shook his head. 'Not enough, and nothing up here to tie it to. And can you abseil, with that leg?'

'Didn't say we were abseiling. I just said we'll use the rope.'

James was absolutely right. Even with two good legs, the rope wasn't long enough for abseiling – it needed to double up so they could pull it down after them.

Beck got the rope out of the bergen and tied one end in a large loop. 'Come here . . . sit down . . .'

James paused for a moment, then shrugged and sat down where Beck had indicated. Beck wrapped the rope loop around his shoulders and threw the other end out of the cave. The single strand just about reached the ground.

'You're going to have to hold my weight,' Beck told James. 'I'll climb down with the rope. Then you chuck it down and climb down on your own. Think you can do that?'

He thought back to a couple of days ago, when he had talked James down the rock face one step at a time, with a lethal drop beneath them. This should be easy, if James remembered what Beck had told him . . .

James flashed a very brief, reluctant smile. 'Yeah, I think so.'

'Cool. Sit with your back against the wall here,

and push your legs against the other side . . .'

James did as he was told, with slightly more enthusiasm. Beck hid a smile. He had often found that when the mind just slumps into gloom, the best cure is to just *do something* with a sense of purpose.

With his back braced against one side of the cave and his legs against the other, James looked solid and immoveable. Beck was prepared to trust his weight to his friend.

And so that was what they did. Beck made his way cautiously over the edge and down the rope. He tried not to put too much weight on it, but sometimes he didn't have a choice. He only had one leg that could take his weight on its own. The occasional grunt or *oof* from above him told him when James was feeling the strain. But he touched down safely and the rope dropped down to land at his feet.

Chapter 27

Five minutes later James was on solid ground next to him. They looked at each other.

'This journey's getting rough, eh?' Beck said.

James answered with a faint smile. 'Hey, if it was easy, anyone could do it.'

'We walk?'

'We walk.' James waved up at the cliff. 'Bye, pandas. Drop in any time.'

Mercifully, finally, the valley began to broaden out. The western side, which had been so steep and sheer, stretched out and became shallower. Trees and bushes returned, safely out of the flood zone. There would be stuff to eat, and wood to burn to make fires.

Beck called a halt and switched on the GPS. James watched silently as he got his bearings. They had made their way down this valley only because they'd been unable to take the route Beck wanted. How off course were they now?

Only a little, as it turned out. Nothing a good half-day's walk couldn't take care of. They would finally be able to leave this wretched valley – and the river that had tried to kill them. Beck opened his mouth to say as much, then thought, and closed it again.

'What?' James asked.

Beck looked down the river, then up the slope, then at James. He held up the GPS. The screen showed a red dot, which was them, then a black line leading from where they were, winding through valleys and over hills, and ending in a large yellow blob.

'That's Sangmu, whoever or whatever Sangmu is. And that's how we reach Lumos. That's when it gets really serious.'

Lumos! The thought that they might actually see the end of the line – even if it was just a glowing line on a screen – filled Beck with hope and energy. He could forget that he was worn out, and soaked, and had a leg that felt like it was about to fall off. *Lumos!*

He looked up at James again. 'You know, this isn't your fight, James. You don't have to do this bit. You can follow the river downstream. You'll soon end up back in civilization. It may take a couple of days, but you know enough to keep yourself alive.'

James expressed his opinion of that with some words that Beck hadn't heard for a long time. Then he added: 'And what do I say when Granddad asks where the hell I've been all this time?'

Beck shrugged. 'Tell him you went off to Nepal to discover yourself, or whatever.'

'Hey, I discovered myself a long time before Nepal. That's why I've come this far and that's why I'm sticking with you. 'Cos it *is* my fight. OK, they didn't kill my parents like they did yours, but they did the next best thing. They drove my dad off . . . my mother would still be alive if they hadn't turned her into a monster . . . and Ian would still be here if . . . if . . .' He swallowed. 'Look, I'm coming, OK?'

Beck bit his lip. Then: 'Thanks,' he whispered quietly. He threw a mock punch. 'C'mon, then. We've got a hot date with Sangmu all lined up.'

Chapter 28

They walked for the rest of the day, and found a spot to camp for the night. The trunk of a pine tree had snapped about a metre from the ground. The trunk lay on the ground, still attached to the stump by a thin sliver of wood, which meant that it was held above the ground with space beneath it. It made a natural shelter for two boys to crawl into, and only a little work was needed to make it comfortable and weather-tight. There was a stream a short distance away and Beck caught them a fish for their supper. They cooked it over a crackling fire of pine needles and shreds of bark, which added a distinct tang to the fresh white meat. They threw its inedible guts and head back into the stream, away from any prowling wildlife, and went to sleep with stomachs full of warm food.

When Beck woke up, he lay there for a while and frowned up at the branches above him. Something seemed to linger inside him – a basic sense that something was unusual and out of place. He couldn't put his finger on it. It lasted while they ate a breakfast of pine nuts and prepared to leave the camp. They had been walking for a couple of hours before it finally dawned on him. What was wrong was that . . . nothing was wrong.

They had a sense of purpose. They knew where they were going. They were in a land that would give them plenty of food and water. Just the amazing sight of the soaring mountains around them made the heart beat stronger.

In short, Beck was *happy*.

And that was how they spent the next couple of days. They walked, they camped, they moved on. They found nuts and berries to supplement their diet of fish. Sometimes they talked, sometimes they bickered in a good-natured way. Usually they walked in companionable silence.

The pain in Beck's leg came and went. Occasionally it was like a third member of the group, throbbing and angry, gnawing into his bones. At those times, he would just grit his teeth and keep walking. Sometimes it went so far away he could almost forget it was there. He was used to aches and pains, and he was used to ignoring them.

He didn't mention any of this to James. It would just worry him. So what if Beck needed medical attention? He wasn't going to get any. They couldn't deviate from their mission in order to go and find a doctor. And so Beck kept his pain private.

The GPS had to be left switched off to save power, so Beck had to keep track of their heading by other means. The sun was one way of doing that. It rose in the east, went round to the south and sank in the west. So, given that it was noon when the sun was at its highest, you knew exactly which way south was. If the time was halfway between noon and sunset, you could see where south-west was – and so on. And both he and James knew the trick of using their watches as a compass – aiming the small hand at the sun, and bisecting the angle between that and the twelve o'clock mark to find north.

A quicker, less precise way was just looking at the

valley slopes. The south-facing ones caught the sun, the north-facing ones often spent their entire lives in shadow. So the plant life on the slopes that faced south was thicker.

Beck kept to the valleys where possible, but sometimes the high ground was impossible to avoid. Nepal mostly *was* high ground, after all. He just had to make sure they didn't linger there.

It wasn't just that it was always warmer and more sheltered down below. It meant fighting gravity less so that they had more strength for travelling. And he was acutely aware of the dangers of altitude sickness. More altitude meant less oxygen. Everyone reacted differently: some people could go up to almost 4000 metres above sea level and not be affected; some could barely make it past 2000 before keeling over. The first signs were usually shortness of breath and dizziness. Maybe with a bit of mental confusion and nausea and a headache for good measure.

Beck knew from experience that he had a good tolerance to altitude. He didn't know how James would react, and James didn't either. So Beck did what he could to keep them low. If they had to climb, he kept a close eye on James for signs of altitude sickness. And he made sure they dressed sensibly, even if it meant stopping several times a day to add or remove clothes, depending on how high or low they were, and whether they needed to conserve warmth or stop themselves overheating.

Neither he nor James had the clothing for really high altitudes. And unlike professional mountain climbers, they had no extra oxygen. If Sangmu was at the top of a big mountain, they were in trouble. That was a problem Beck would deal with when it arose.

The high ground still had its uses, as long as you didn't get caught up there at night. You could get a general idea of the lie of the land, so you didn't have to keep retracing your steps. You could keep an eye out for landmarks and judge how well you were maintaining your course. You could look down on the obstacles along your route, and make a mental map of the best way to get from A to B. And you could see the weather coming, just in case the rain had any repeat performances scheduled.

At the bottom of every valley was a stream or river, and every one had fish. They made sure to finish each day with a cooked meal. It was always fish, roasted on a stick, with something else – nuts or berries – on the side. The instant noodles were finally used up so they moved on to the soft white inner bark of pine trees, and seeds from the cones. But still they felt hungry. They were using up a lot more energy than they could replace and the hunger pangs were a constant companion.

Sometimes Beck and James discussed what food they would eat if they got out of this adventure alive. They veered between a big juicy steak, a plate of cheese, and chocolate bars. It's funny what you crave when you're hungry. The feeling of a stomach full of warm food was hard to beat, and it had been a while now since they'd had that.

Chapter 29

Eventually they came down off a plateau into a high valley. The sole occupants were a herd of gaur cows, which moved away grumpily as the boys came close. They were half the size again of a normal farm cow. Their skin was sleek and glossy over moving slabs of muscle, their horns curved and pointed, maybe half a metre long. Even though the animals seemed placid, the horns made the point that they could look after themselves.

None of these cows would be called Daisy, James said with a laugh.

They grazed the grass thoughtfully, and every now and then one would twitch its tail to disturb a small cloud of buzzing flies. They kept a watchful eye on the two boys who had decided to share their valley.

A stream ran rapidly past them and then disappeared: Beck could hear the sound of a waterfall. He and James stopped and looked over the drop. The water tumbled down through a series of ledges and pools. It wasn't steep – they could get down it easily, even with Beck's leg, which continued to throb.

'Lunch first,' Beck said firmly.

They sat down and James peeled off his boots to let his feet breathe. He kept his socks on to conserve the warmth in his body, wiggling his toes underneath the wool. 'We must really stink,' he said happily.

Beck grinned and had to agree. Apart from their dunking in the river, it had been a long time since they'd had a proper shower.

James broke out their stored supply of pine nuts and Himalayan candy, then gave Beck a nudge. 'Maybe it's time for that steak?' he quipped, nodding towards the cows.

The nearest one gazed back with a look that said, *Try it, mate*.

'They're sacred in Nepal,' Beck said. 'It's illegal to kill them – unless you're a lot more desperate than we are.'

'Whatever. How about these?' James got up and in socked feet went over to a clump of bushes. He appeared to have found some berries. He pulled back a branch decorated with purple flowers to let Beck see the cluster of bright red blobs.

'We don't know they're not poisonous,' Beck cautioned. Red berries came under the 'maybe' category. Black and blue were usually safe – they had already found some of those; white and yellow were usually not; and red – you never knew. You had to proceed carefully: first rub some of the flesh on your skin to see if there was any kind of reaction. Then wait a few hours. If there was no rash or stinging, then take a tiny bit of the juice and touch it to your lips. And so on, until finally you got to eat a bit and waited again. To do this properly could take days, and on their timescale, it wasn't worth the risk.

'Trust me,' Beck told James, 'you don't want to get poisoned out here. We have other food sources. Think of the big picture. Stay healthy. Get Lumos. Survive.'

James hobbled back in his socks, and Beck decided to let his own feet have some air. As he reached for the laces, he had to force his injured leg to bend – he hoped James hadn't heard his grunt of pain.

James had, and was immediately at his side. 'That sounded bad. How is it?'

'It's . . .' Beck knew that they had to be able to trust each other and he didn't want to lie. 'It's not good,' he admitted. 'It's painful and swollen and it isn't healing. It just needs a rest.'

'You should change the bandage again.'

James didn't sound like he was going to accept an argument. Beck sighed and wriggled out of his trousers so that James could get at the bandage around his thigh.

James winced. The white gauze was stained brown with crusted blood. 'You shouldn't have let it get like this.'

Beck shrugged. 'I'm, like, full of this red stuff, and when my skin gets a hole in it, it comes leaking out. I'm funny that way.'

James frowned at him. 'OK, well, at least let me change it . . .'

The old blood had glued the bandage to Beck's

skin. James had to soak it in water before he could peel it off. He went white, and even Beck, who had suspected what they might find, was shocked.

On either side of the gash made by the bear's claw, Beck's leg was badly swollen. The skin was dark red and inflamed, and stretched so tight it looked like it might burst if James pricked it with a pin.

But the wound itself was dark, black and jagged. It wasn't just the clotted blood – some of it was the flesh itself. It was dark and rotten, and it smelled bad.

Beck had seen this before. Or rather, he had seen the after-effects. Without proper treatment, this would turn into gangrene.

He could lose his leg, and without help he could lose his life.

Chapter 30

'Oh, *man*!' James exclaimed. 'How did it get like that?'

'Had some mountains to walk over.' Beck bit his lip. He hadn't expected it to look that bad.

'Well,' James said doubtfully, 'we can probably— Hey, get away!'

A couple of flies from the cloud that hung around the cows had ventured further and settled on Beck's wound like squat, black little aliens. They immediately buzzed off out of range of James's hand.

Beck swallowed. 'No, leave them.'

James stared at him. 'Eh?'

'Let them be,' said Beck. 'I want them to lay eggs.'

'B-but . . .' James spluttered. 'Eggs will hatch

maggots! You'll have maggots in . . . in . . .' He waved a helpless hand at the wound.

'This is rotten, and maggots eat rotten flesh,' Beck told him. 'At the moment the rotten flesh is all on the outside. If the rot goes in, if it gets into my bloodstream – then I'm good as dead. I'll get blood poisoning and gangrene. So, let 'em be. They'll soon produce maggots, which will start eating. They'll swallow up all the dead flesh and pus. Once I start to see fresh blood – then I'll know they've dealt with it.'

He didn't add, *I hope*. This felt like the hardest thing Beck had ever done. He had swallowed all kinds of creatures in his time, but he had never knowingly let them get inside his skin, lay eggs, breed . . .

Still, he had seen it done. He and his Uncle Al had visited a friend in hospital. The friend had suffered a bad case of frostbite in the Arctic. Part of his feet had turned black and gangrenous. He had risked losing his legs. Instead, the doctors had gone for the maggot treatment. And it had worked. The little wrigglers had nibbled away the rotten flesh, one tiny bite at a time. Small chunks of his feet and toes were missing, but he could walk and he was alive.

The same thing should work here. *Should*, Beck thought to himself.

A couple more flies had settled as he spoke. Presumably the word was going out in the fly community that there was a pleasant alternative to cows.

'How will you know when they've laid their eggs?' James asked.

'I'm not sure, but we should just leave them for a while.'

'You sit there, then. I'll boil some water . . .' James tore his gaze away and stood up. He cast a final look back. 'Y' know, that wound's quite high up inside your leg.'

'Yeah?'

'So, um, how high up will the maggots, um, eat . . .'

'They eat rotten flesh,' Beck said firmly. 'Nothing else.'

'Nothing?'

'Nothing.'

'OK, OK, just saying.' James trudged over to the stream to collect some water.

They ate their lunch and washed it down with pine-needle tea. After that, Beck decided that the flies had had their chance. James helped bandage his leg up again and Beck pulled his trousers on.

'Ladies and gentlemen,' James announced, 'roll up for Beck Granger and his Marvellous Munching Maggots . . .'

He was reaching down to help Beck up when an angry squeal echoed around the valley. Something heavy came charging through the trees towards them. Branches waved and cracked. For a moment Beck had a ridiculous flashback to the rhinos he had seen in Africa.

But there wouldn't be a rhino halfway up a mountain in Nepal . . .

There wasn't, but it was almost as bad. Half a ton of beef burst out into the open. A very large, very angry bull, its eyes fixed firmly on them.

Neither of the boys had given much thought to the fact that where there were cows, there would also be a bull.

It pawed the ground and snorted. In bull talk, it was basically saying, *Clear off, and fast*.

'My, we're big, aren't we?' Beck whispered calmly. He slipped the bergen straps over his shoulders, slowly, without any sudden movements. The bull snorted again and took a step closer.

'If it charges,' Beck continued quietly, 'you go left, I'll go right. It can't get both of us at once.'

'No, it can get both of us, one after the other.'

'Got a better idea?'

'No . . .'

The bull tossed its head and its horns flashed in the sun. They looked like an afterthought – something the bull had put on like Beck might put on a pair of earphones. They curved out on either side, almost as wide as Beck's outstretched arms, each ending in a vicious point.

The bull lowered its head until those two points were aiming right at them, and then it charged.

'Go!' Beck yelled, and they leaped away in opposite directions.

Leaping was a mistake. The moment the weight was transferred to Beck's bad leg, he felt pain spear up into his thigh. His leg crumpled and he ploughed into the grass.

Even as he fell, he was desperately twisting round to face the bull. He had to get away.

But it was still coming towards him, head down, those powerful, sharp horns barely metres away . . .

Chapter 31

A flash across his vision. A fleeting glimpse of spotted fur and a sleek, lithe body. A hiss, a furious yowl, an angry bellow . . .

All Beck knew was that the bull wasn't charging at him any more. He grabbed the opportunity to scramble to his feet, making sure that his leg didn't let him down again.

James was beside him, helping him up. 'Blimey. It just came out of nowhere – right out of the trees – look at that!'

Beck risked looking back at what sounded like a pitched battle.

His rescuer was a snow leopard – three times the size of a large house cat, forty kilos of muscle and claws and teeth. The bull had its head lowered and one of those horns could have run the leopard through, but the leopard wasn't going to let it get near. It hissed and bared its teeth and danced lightly on its powerful paws. Whenever it lunged forward, the bull retreated. Sometimes the bull would take a swing with its head, but the leopard always sprang nimbly away before the horn reached it. Bit by bit, lunge by lunge, the two battling animals were moving away from the boys. The other cows huddled together, well away from the big cat with the fangs, seeking safety in numbers.

As they watched, the leopard took a final spring, over the bull's head and onto its back. The bull bellowed and bucked but the leopard clung onto its powerful shoulders, its claws drawing blood.

They were evenly matched. The bull had strength and staying power, the leopard had agility and powerful jaws. But Beck didn't want to hang around to see who won.

'Let's get out of here – and fast,' he said quietly.

For the next hour the boys kept moving as fast as they possibly could.

The leopard had spooked them to their core, and they realized how close they had come to disaster. Out in these mountains they weren't top of the food chain.

From the high valley with the cows and the leopard, they made their way down beside the waterfall to another river plain. Still off the tourist track, still with barely any other creatures about. Just James and Beck, two specks of humanity surrounded by the immensity of the Himalayan peaks.

Beck's leg, though, was already feeling a little better. It might have been the fact that James had changed the bandage. Or that the leopard and the bull had taken his mind off it. Or maybe that the flies had laid their eggs and lots of new little friends were down there, munching their way through the infection . . . Time would tell.

Finally they came to the river. The only crossing place – without making a huge detour – seemed to be a line of boulders that ran almost from bank to bank.

James went first, leaping from one to the other while the water rushed by beneath him. Then he tied one end of the rope around himself and threw the other back to Beck. James stood secure on the far bank and slowly reeled Beck in as he jumped across carefully, one stone at a time, making sure his injured leg could handle each leap.

On the other side, they filled up the water bottle, then walked for another couple of hours, up the valley, away from the river's mosquitoes. They stopped to make camp just inside the tree line, where there was shelter from the cool breezes that blew down from the mountains.

James built another fire and Beck fought the temptation to peek under his bandage. If the maggots were there, he didn't want to know. If they weren't, there was nothing he could do about it.

Dinner was the usual fare of fish, followed by nuts and berries and Himalayan candy. Beck switched on the GPS and pursed his lips in satisfaction. The red spot that showed their position and the yellow blob that was Sangmu were very close.

'Tomorrow,' he said. 'We will get there tomorrow.'

James just nodded, his mouth full of pine nuts.

Beck gazed down the valley, back the way they had come. It was already shrouded in night. When he twisted round, the way ahead was lit a dull red by the setting sun.

It seemed fitting. There was no going back. Not now.

Chapter 32

The next morning they rose again, saying very little. They had grown used to working as a team, understanding what needed doing without speaking. They dowsed the fire by peeing on it – there was no point in wasting good drinking water; but they always ensured that not even a spark could escape into the dry pine needles that lay around it.

Forest fires were always a danger; moreover, any fire would betray their presence. Beck's dad had once told him, 'It only takes a spark . . .' According to his dad, this applied to life and survival and spirit as well as to forest fires. Beck had always remembered that: a little spark could be just enough to keep you going.

After another hour they had left the trees behind

them. Beck saw what was ahead and faltered for a moment. He hadn't wanted to do this . . .

But he had no choice. He gave the GPS a final check to be sure. Yup – they were going up onto high ground, and staying there. No more coming down into the valleys to shelter. By the time evening came, they would be well above the trees, maybe even above the snow line. It would be a completely different ballgame.

But they had made their choice. If they were to reach Sangmu, then the only way was up.

They set their faces towards the high ground, and climbed.

For the rest of the day Nepal seemed to fall away beneath them, but there were always mountains ahead. Beck knew they were climbing higher than ever before and all his worries about altitude came flooding back.

Food, water, shelter – all three times harder to find here than down below.

The cold dry wind both dehydrated you and made you hypothermic.

And the oxygen – or rather, the lack of it.

The worst thing about oxygen starvation was that you didn't realize it was happening. As long as you were breathing something, your body stopped noticing it wasn't getting much in return. Beck had watched videos of pilots training for high altitudes. Their oxygen was turned off and they were told to do normal things like put wooden shapes into holes or count up to ten. They couldn't do it, and they couldn't even work out that something was wrong.

That was what frightened Beck the most. He was breaking the most important survival rule he knew – he was actively heading into danger. And his oxygen-starved brain might not be able to spot it before it was too late. In the training films they always turned the oxygen back on, and five minutes later the pilots could have a good laugh, watching themselves act like zombies on video.

If they hadn't turned the oxygen on again, then very soon the pilots would have passed out. Then their brains would have died, shortly followed by the rest of them.

And that was exactly what might lie ahead for

Beck and James, if either of them got bad altitude sickness and couldn't get help.

But . . . Sangmu beckoned, so they kept going.

Nepal's fertile slopes and thick forests were far behind and far below them. They walked over rocky ground scoured clean and dry by the wind. The snow line came ever closer, now only a few hundred metres above them. They were dressed in every piece of clothing they had. Warm hats kept their body heat from flowing out of the top of their heads. Sunglasses protected their eyes from ultraviolet rays that could fry their retinas. As long as they kept moving, they were warm.

However, as the day drew on, Beck knew that they would have to start thinking about shelter.

They might be forced to simply bed down beside a big boulder, out of the wind, huddled together to share warmth. Another thought struck him and he cocked an eye up at the snow. Maybe they should head up there and dig a snow shelter; a cave in the snow that would keep them as snug as they liked? He had done that with Tikaani in Alaska and it had saved their lives.

But even climbing to where there was enough snow, and then digging out the shelter, would take time and energy they couldn't spare. So his eyes started to scan the barren landscape for somewhere else . . .

Chapter 33

They turned a corner and suddenly found themselves looking down on a small village.

For a long time they both stood and stared down at it, not quite believing it was there.

'Wow,' James said eventually.

Beck pulled out the GPS. The battery level was in the red, but their red dot was slap bang on top of Sangmu's yellow blob. This was where they were meant to be.

Right here.

It was obviously an old Sherpa village and it lay hidden away in a small valley. It must have been protected from the wind because there were even a few scrubby fields scattered around it. The low buildings were built of grey stone and timber, battered and worn by the weather. But they were cared for. It didn't look much, but someone had to live there. The houses were clustered together in a sheltered hollow to one side of the valley.

All at once the boys spotted a lone figure walking along a track that led up the valley and into the village. They looked at each other, then headed down the slope to intercept him.

'Hello!' James called as they approached.

The man stopped and stared. Tourists were obviously a rarity here. A wizened brown face peered at them with suspicion and surprise out of the depths of a colourful woollen hat.

And that was when Beck remembered he didn't speak a word of any of the local languages.

'We're looking for Lumos,' James said. Another blank look. 'Lumos? Lu – mos?' He clearly assumed that foreigners would always understand English so long as you spoke slowly enough.

'Sangmu,' Beck said. 'We're looking for Sangmu.'

There was a flicker of recognition in the man's eyes. 'Sangmu?' He obviously thought it odd that two

European boys should pop up in his village out of nowhere, looking for Sangmu.

'Sangmu! Yes!' James nodded vigorously. 'Ye-e-s. Can – you – take – us – to – Sang – mu.'

'Sangmu . . .' the man said again, and rolled his eyes expressively. 'Sangmu!' He gave his head a jerk towards the village, to indicate that they should follow him.

There were very few people around. Those still out and about gave them surprised looks. They followed the dirt track between low houses and the man rapped on a wooden door halfway along. He called out something and a woman's voice answered from inside. He pushed the door open and indicated they should go in.

The room had a low ceiling and a very welcome fire that roared away in an iron brazier, filling the place with warmth. A girl only a few years older than Beck and James was stirring a cooking pot. She looked up in surprise at her two visitors. The man spoke to her in rapid words that neither boy could follow, apart from 'Sangmu' – a word which she repeated in disbelief.

Finally the man bowed himself out of the room.

'Sangmu,' he said, pointing at the girl, and closed the door behind him.

She put her fingers to her chest. 'I am Sangmu. I am sorry; if you want my mother, she is midwifing in another village.'

Beck felt a huge gush of relief to find that she spoke English. 'No, no, it's you we want,' he assured her. 'Um. I think.' He and James looked at each other. Where to start? This wasn't a moment they had prepared for.

'Um. It's kind of a long story . . .' He pulled off his hat, with an instinctive shake of his head to untangle his hair. 'We, uh, came here because . . .'

But she was staring at him as though she had seen a ghost. Slowly, tentatively, she came forward, not taking her eyes off his.

Beck stood still, puzzled.

Sangmu slowly reached out and touched his face, then felt a strand of his hair.

'Beck. You are Beck Granger, no?'

Chapter 34

The two boys and Sangmu sat huddled in front of the fire. Beck cradled a mug of warming broth in both hands and listened like he had never listened before.

Sangmu began her story: 'I heard the explosion. Who could not? It echoed around the mountains. It was ten years ago but I still remember seeing fire falling out of the night. It came down behind the ridge.

'I was only a small girl, but even I knew it could only be an aeroplane.

'The next morning some of our herders went to where they thought the wreckage must have landed. To everyone's surprise, they brought back with them a badly injured Western woman. They had found the wreckage scattered across the slopes, but she had still been strapped into a seat. She was in a terrible state, and no one thought she would live. Many broken bones, and internal injuries, and burns from the explosion. But she was still alive. They brought her to my father, the doctor. He decided that all he could do was make her comfortable until she died. He could not make her better but he could take her pain away.

'For two days I helped them. I remember wiping her brow and putting water in her mouth – even a small child could do that. The next day, I was alone – and she opened her eyes.

'Her voice was very faint but I could hear her, and I spoke a little English. There was so much I did not understand but I understood enough.

'She knew she had survived a crash and she knew she was dying. She told me her name – Melanie Granger. She asked after her husband, David. I could only tell her, "No David." Our herders had found no sign of him. And I thought she was asking about someone called Beck. I said, "No Beck," but then I realized that she was not asking, she was telling me about him. Her son.

'She asked for her things. My parents had undressed her to put her to bed, but we had kept everything. I found her clothes and she told me to look in the pockets. I found a small device. I did not know what it was then, but now I know it was a hard drive. She told me it must go to David's brother, Alan Granger, in England. She made me promise.

'I was only a little girl – what could I do? I vowed I would do what I could. And soon after that, she closed her eyes for the last time.'

Beck had tears trickling down his cheeks now; he rubbed his eyes, trying to stop himself. James put a hand on Beck's shoulder.

'I knew that one day I would meet you, Beck,' Sangmu went on. 'It has been a feeling I have had ever since your mother died.'

'So . . . what happened to the hard drive?' Beck asked.

Her face clouded. 'I decided that I would tell my father about it. He had been educated abroad and he would know what to do. He might know how to find this Alan Granger.

'But that night I was woken up by someone moving

in our downstairs room. He was very quiet. I only heard because I too slept downstairs, in the pantry next door. So I could not wake my parents without the intruder knowing. I peered through the door.

'It was a man, another Westerner – big and powerful, with thick dark hair. And I saw that he had a gun at his side, so I was terrified and hid. I watched him from under my bed.

'He was large but he knew how to move quietly. I watched him go swiftly through the room. Everything was put back exactly as it had been, but not a thing escaped his gaze. And he found the hard drive. Immediately he stopped looking – it was what he wanted. And he left as quietly as he had come.

'I was almost in tears. I had made a vow to a dying woman! I wanted to call my parents, to call anyone – one scream from me and the whole village would have come running. But he had that gun. How many might he kill with it before we got the drive back?

'So instead, I pulled on my clothes and I followed him.

'It was easy to do – the night was clear, the moon was half full so there was plenty of light, and I knew the roads. I knew them better than he did. Several times I saw him stumble in the dark, and I learned some English words that I never repeated to my parents.

'And it soon became clear where he was going. There is a monastery in the next valley. We all knew that some rich Westerner had bought it and made it his home. No one was allowed in now – it was surrounded by guards. Other Westerners came and went by plane – we never saw them in the village, but the villagers sold them food. I had been there a few times when we took them supplies, so I knew the way.

'And that meant I knew the shortcuts. Where the road bends round a cliff, I could cut across the higher ground and be there first. Soon I saw him coming below me. I jumped on him.

'I can laugh now – one small girl against a large man! And he laughed too, as he easily beat me off and held me down with the barrel of the gun at my head. I did not care. I was crying – not because of him but because I would not be able to keep my promise.

'He asked me my name. I told him. I also told him he was a thief and I told him the hard drive was not his. He told me that if I was an adult he would have killed me for what I had seen. But instead, I should forget that any of this had happened, and run on home.

'And so I did. But every day I ask Melanie to forgive me, because I could not honour her last request.'

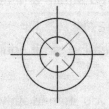

Chapter 35

Beck and James sat in stunned silence. Both of them blinked a few times to get rid of tears that neither would admit to.

'Ian . . .' James was the first to speak. 'The man must have been Ian.'

Beck couldn't care less about Ian. He now knew what had happened to his mother.

Mostly. Some bits were just too unbelievable. . .

'She survived an exploding plane? Still in her seat?'

Sangmu could only shrug.

'It's happened before,' James said quietly. 'I read about a Czech woman who survived when her plane exploded ten kilometres up: she was pinned inside the wreckage as it fell. The pieces absorbed the impact.' Beck stared at him and he shrugged. 'Hey, weird stuff interests me.'

OK, Beck conceded, so it could happen. But to his own mum?

'I recognized you immediately, Beck,' Sangmu said with a little smile. 'Your face is the same shape as hers.'

'What happened to my mother's body?' he asked in a whisper.

Sangmu took him gently by the hand and led him to the mantelpiece. His eyes fell on a jewelled box that stood alone. It was almost like a shrine, with a small candle on either side.

'She was cremated. We did not know her religion but our priest said the words he thought would be appropriate. I collected her ashes. They are here. I give her honour each day' – she paused – 'in place of my broken promise.'

Mama! A word Beck hadn't said in ten years. It almost tore its way out of his throat.

'Please, don't touch that.' Sangmu had suddenly switched her attention to James. An old army revolver hung in a leather holster pinned to a wall and he was fingering it thoughtfully. 'That was my grandfather's. It was his when he fought with the British Army.'

'Sorry.' James took his hand away.

'And what about my father?' Beck asked in a whisper.

Sangmu shook her head. 'I am sorry, Beck. We never found your father. The men looked, when I told them about him, but . . . no. I myself trekked up to where the crash happened – it is not far – but . . .' She shook her head with a puzzled smile, as though she could not believe the memory. 'There was a small family of snow leopards there. They seemed to be living in the wreckage – they thought it was a cave . . . I could not get close.'

Beck had to force the words out. 'Thanks for trying.'

He thought of his father's body lying in a crevasse somewhere, covered with snow and ice for all eternity. Lying in the embrace of the mighty Himalayas with a mountain as his tombstone. A solitary tear rolled down his cheek. How he longed just to hold his father's hand, one more time.

'Beck.' James's voice broke harshly into his

trance, and Beck remembered that he wasn't the only one learning something new about a parent figure. 'This hard drive Sangmu mentioned . . . it must be what Ian was coming for. He was going to get it back.'

'What could be on it?'

'Who knows? Something your mother wanted taken to your uncle. Something my granddad thought was important enough to kill for. Beck, this is all about the hard drive!' James's eyes began to shine with excitement. 'And it's at the monastery! We can go and get it!'

Beck thought, then shook his head. 'If I was Edwin Blake and I got hold of a hard drive full of stuff that could incriminate me, I'd destroy it. Why keep it hanging around for the next ten years?'

James shrugged. 'Ian thought different. He must have had a reason to think it was still there.' He turned to Sangmu. 'This monastery, have you ever been in?'

She shook her head. 'They are very private. Even when we deliver food, we leave it in the storehouse at the foot of the steps for them to pick up later. No, I have never been inside.'

'When are you delivering the next lot?'

'Tomorrow.'

'Right.' James started to think out loud. 'We hitch a ride with Sangmu. We – I dunno – we disguise ourselves as Sherpas, right, and . . .' Beck and Sangmu smiled at each other. 'What?' he asked indignantly.

'Neither of us is ever going to look like a Sherpa,' Beck said. 'Look, first thing is to take a look at the place. Then we'll decide on a way in . . .'

Chapter 36

James whistled. 'Wow.'

He and Beck lay side by side at the top of a rocky ridge and gazed across the valley. The monastery was worth a whistle.

It was a collection of tall, soaring white buildings, topped with flat red tile roofs and patterned with gold leaf. It seemed to cling to the side of a mountain. There was a sheer rock face beneath it, descending all the way to the valley floor. An equally sheer one rose above it and disappeared into the low clouds. It looked like it was glued to the cliff, though when Beck studied it closely he could see that it was actually built on a very narrow ridge.

At one end the ridge angled steeply down towards the valley. There were steps carved into the slope. That was the only way anyone who wasn't a mountaineer could get in or out.

Sangmu had mentioned the steps, and a store-house at the foot. Beck peered more closely. There it was – a small hut. Could they get that near? It would be somewhere to hide . . .

A security fence ran down the middle of the valley, from one end to the other. There was a guard post where the dirt track from Sangmu's village cut through it. Beyond that, the track led up to the foot of the steps.

Also on the other side of the fence, a brand-new tarmac airstrip had been carved into the flat valley floor. At one end the ground fell away. At the other stood a small metal hangar, with a couple of air-craft parked outside. The track bent to go round the hangar and on towards the end of the airstrip.

'I've only seen pictures of this place,' James said. 'Never seen it in real life. It looks even better than I imagined. Wow! It's like a royal palace, isn't it?'

Beck grunted. Sangmu had told them its history. Once there had been a monk, a holy man, living there. He had attracted a small community of followers who lived in a network of caves, both natural ones and others that they had carved out themselves. Eventually, as the group grew, they built the monastery over the site. It had thrived for a thousand years, but bit by bit the religious community had dwindled until there were only a couple of geriatric monks left. They had been happy to sell up to the crazy Westerner who wanted this place as a home, and move elsewhere.

Now, everything was sealed away behind guards and barbed wire.

So typical of Lumos, Beck thought. Take a place of beauty, a holy place dedicated to goodness, and use it to conceal the secrets of one wicked, selfish old man.

But Edwin Blake must feel secure here. If the hard drive really was still around, it would probably not be tucked away. He would feel no need to be secretive. If they could get in, they stood a good chance of finding it.

Not that it would be easy. The monastery might only be the size of a small village, but that was still a lot of rooms. However, room by room, inch by inch,

Beck thought, he would search it and locate what he wanted . . .

Suddenly James was clutching his elbow. 'Look! Look!' He was pointing at the aeroplanes at the end of the runway. Beck looked, but couldn't see anything in particular. A small propeller-driven plane – a two-seater – and a fancy executive jet.

'What?'

'That jet! That's Granddad's plane! His private one!' James swivelled his head back to gaze at the monastery in awe. 'Means he's here.'

Beck scowled across the valley. OK, that was not good news. Not that he'd mind confronting Edwin Blake one day. But not right now. Right now, Blake's presence meant extra security. That would make their job harder.

He bit his lip. 'OK. First thing is to get in. Second is to avoid him . . .'

'Why should we want to avoid him?' James asked in an odd voice.

Beck frowned and looked round, and his eyes went wide as he found himself staring down the barrel of a gun.

It was the gun from Sangmu's house – the old revolver belonging to her grandfather.

'James,' he gasped, 'what . . . ?'

James pulled back on the hammer with his thumb. The gun clicked as it was primed to shoot. 'I'm taking you in, Granger.'

Chapter 37

'Really bad idea,' Beck whispered as the barrier loomed ahead. The guards sat up and took notice as the two boys approached. No doubt they imagined they were dealing with two slightly lost tourists.

'Shut up and keep walking . . .'

They were at the barrier, and a large man with a sub-machine gun slung over one shoulder blocked their way.

'Private property.' He spoke in English but with a strong middle European accent. 'Even if you're lost—'

And then, as James produced the pistol from behind Beck, he jumped back in shock, bringing his gun to bear. But James merely prodded the end of the barrel against Beck's skull, behind his ear. He spoke loudly and clearly.

'My name is James Blake, my grandfather is Edwin Blake, and trust me, he will be *so* angry if you don't let us in.'

After that, it didn't take long . . .

First the guards put a call through to the monastery. Beck couldn't make out what the voice at the other end was saying, but it was fast and furious and it made the guard go white. Immediately they were bundled into a Jeep and driven towards the monastery steps. One of the guards took the opportunity to relieve James, gently, of the pistol. He was as uneasy at the thought of a gun being wielded by an over-enthusiastic teenager as Beck was.

It made no difference. Beck was still a captive.

Several times he tried to meet James's eye and work out if this was for real. James had been raised by a professional assassin. It had once been his life's ambition to kill Beck. He had changed sides once before in his life. And Beck knew from experience that he was capable of making some really bad decisions . . .

Whether or not James really was taking him in, as far as Beck was concerned, this had all just gone bad – very bad. And there seemed no possible good outcome to this scenario.

But James was carefully avoiding his eye, and Beck had no way of really knowing. The other boy had his head turned to look at the monastery, so Beck did likewise.

The plus side of James's action meant that he would soon be in there. The minus was, Beck wondered if he would ever get to leave.

The complex of buildings towered above them on the ridge. Dusk was coming down on the valley, and the rows and rows of shuttered windows were like shining beacons. The walls were all steep and smooth. It would surely be impossible to escape down one.

At one end of the monastery there was a flat terrace set into the mountainside. A single figure leaned on the balustrade and looked down at them. Even though he was just a speck, something about the stance suggested ownership. Possession. That man up there was in total charge of this whole place. Surely, Beck thought, it was Edwin Blake.

Beck kept his face expressionless as he looked

up at him. He would not show fear. Even if this was the last five minutes of his life, he would stick to the principles he believed in. Goodness and trust. Blake could kill him, but never defeat him.

The Jeep halted next to the storehouse and they were ushered up the stone staircase towards the monastery. Warm, dry air and bright electric light hit them as they entered through the double wooden doors. The original woodwork must have been ornate and wonderfully bright. Now it had been painted over with bland colours, and the stone floor was covered with thick carpet. It reminded Beck of a flash hotel. It must have cost a fortune to get all this stuff in. For precisely that reason, as far as Beck was concerned, it was tacky. It was showing off: *Woo, look how rich I am!*

They were led along twisting passages and up flights of stairs, climbing ever higher inside the complex. Beck's sense of direction told him that they were heading towards the same end of the monastery as the terrace.

And sure enough, they ended up in a huge room, at one end a glass wall with a sliding door opening onto the terrace. The room was dominated by a roaring fire in the middle. The chairs were soft and comfortable. One section of wall was taken up with a single massive flatscreen and a host of smaller ones around it, all showing news channels or streams of data. The rest of the walls were covered with portraits or sculptures. Yet there was a coldness that pervaded the room and sent a chill down Beck's spine.

And there was the man himself.

In all the pictures Beck had seen of Edwin Blake, he was wearing a grey business suit. Here he wore a knitted jumper and jeans. The outfit looked casual, but Beck noticed the expensive Italian leather loafers on his feet. The old man was tall and thin, with a fringe of white hair around a bald head.

The guards withdrew at a signal Beck didn't see, and then there was just him, and James . . . and the man who had dominated his life, who had killed his parents, who stood for everything Beck despised.

Edwin Blake came slowly towards them with a broad smile on his skull-like face.

Chapter 38

Blake had his hands in his pockets, his head tilted quizzically.

'James? This is a surprise in so many ways. And . . . you have indeed brought someone who looks a lot like Beck Granger.'

He walked slowly around the two of them, reminding Beck uncomfortably of a shark circling its prey. James turned to keep track of him. Beck simply stood and stared straight ahead. He couldn't help but flinch when he felt Blake's fingers run through his hair. He failed to stifle a gasp as the man suddenly tore a clump of it out.

'Dark roots. Beck Granger a bottle-blond – who would have thought?'

Blake came round to the front. Long, probing

fingers grabbed Beck's chin and pushed his head back so that the old man could look him in the eye. Beck did all he could to return the stare without blinking. Blake's face twisted into a sneer. He let go of Beck and stepped away.

'Either Beck Granger has a twin that I've never heard of – or this is indeed him. How interesting. How many questions does this raise?' He started to circle them again. 'I suppose the first is . . . James, why exactly aren't you at school? I pay good money to have you educated at that college.'

'Um . . .' It was a very logical question, but clearly not one James had expected. 'Ian took me out.'

'Ah yes, Ian . . . And that is the second question. Ian very definitely told me that Beck Granger was dead . . .' He frowned. 'No, I tell a lie. He told me that he'd *heard* Beck die. Heard the screams, found a torn and bloodied T-shirt which I saw myself . . .'

'Ian thought Beck might have faked it,' James said. He was sounding more confident now. 'He tracked him down and found him in Johannesburg. Then he got me out of school so that I could befriend him and bring him here.'

Beck's mind whirled with the betrayal, the deceit. Had James really done that?

'And where is Ian now?'

James swallowed. 'Beck sabotaged his rope. He fell.'

His grandfather hesitated, and took in the obvious pain on James's face. 'Commiserations. You probably haven't been keeping up with the news, but the authorities have indeed found the body of an adult Caucasian male at the bottom of a mountain. And it does seem that his rope was cut. Why didn't you just kill Beck in return? You must have had the opportunity.'

James's mouth worked silently for a moment. 'I . . . thought you might like to see—'

'You *thought*,' his grandfather sneered. 'You thought nothing. You're still weak, boy. Didn't have the guts to do it yourself?'

James flushed. 'If I still had the gun, I'd do it here and now to prove it to you!'

'Here?' Blake asked mildly. He looked down at the very expensive carpet. 'No, I don't think so. Out on the terrace, perhaps. Easier to clean up afterwards.'

He stepped back and observed Beck thoughtfully. 'Beck, you are limping. Hurt your leg?'

In a flash, he lashed out with one foot and caught Beck squarely on his wound. Beck was taken by surprise, and shouted out in pain as he crumpled to the floor.

'Kick him, James,' Blake ordered.

James hesitated only a moment before drawing back his foot, and Beck knew he was going to do it. He curled up as tightly as he could to protect his injury, but James's foot caught him full on the shin of his injured leg. Beck moaned through clenched teeth as he clutched it.

'You have five seconds to be standing before I do it again,' Blake said coldly.

Beck had no doubt he meant it, and staggered to his feet. His eyes were streaming and he wiped them with his fist.

'That's better. I couldn't help noticing a certain disrespect in your demeanour, Beck. I advise you to lose it. It's really not in your best interests.' Suddenly the cold had vanished and Blake sounded almost warm and friendly – an elderly uncle trying to entertain his two nephews. 'Come over here, boys. I've got some-thing that might interest you both . . .'

He led the way over to a display case set into the wall next to the terrace window. Outside, Beck noticed, the paving disappeared into the gloom of the evening.

In front of them, the series of glass shelves housed a random collection of objects that didn't really match the décor of the rest of the room. Some of these bits and pieces couldn't have been worth anything. A battered passport. Coins. A circuit board.

But on the top shelf there was a framed photo-graph, and Beck immediately realized what this was all about. The photo showed Abby Blake. It had been taken on one of her better days. A smiling, happy, laughing face that showed nothing of the person she had really been. This was like a shrine to Abby.

'Your mother had a career that took her all over the world,' Blake was saying to James, who was staring at the display, transfixed. 'She always brought back a little memento from each mission. Sometimes I amuse myself remembering what she did on each occasion. She was a daughter to be proud of. You could learn from her.'

Beck continued to scan the shelves. Each piece had been selected by Abby – therefore it had been important to her mission in some way. He felt a morbid fascination in trying to work out why.

A small glass bottle. Had she poisoned someone? A silk scarf. What did that mean?

And then his eyes lighted on a single object sitting on the middle shelf. A slightly battered-looking portable hard drive.

Edwin Blake touched a button and the glass door to the terrace slid silently aside. Cold air blew into the room, and lights came on automatically to illuminate the paving and the balustrade. Beyond them, the dark night was now impenetrable.

Edwin reached casually into an alcove, and suddenly there was a gun in his hand, pointing straight at Beck. 'Step outside, Beck,' he ordered.

Chapter 39

Beck stepped slowly out onto the terrace, followed by James and his grandfather.

So this was it. Edwin Blake had already said that the terrace would be the place to shoot someone. Would he do it himself? Or would he give the gun to James so that he could make good his boast?

He found himself hoping that it would be Blake. It felt odd, but he really didn't want it to be James. James could still change his mind. He could still find a way in life that was right. It was never too late to come good.

'Stand over there, Beck.' With a jerk of the barrel, Blake pointed at a red tile set into the floor by the balustrade. 'Look out into the night.'

Beck stood his ground and spoke for the first time

since his capture. 'If you're going to shoot me, you can look me in the eye and do it.'

'Shoot you?' Blake frowned, then suddenly laughed. 'Shoot you? What a waste! No, I'm not – yet – going to do that. You may beg me to, one day . . . But not right now.' He tucked the gun into his waistband and held up both hands. 'There! See? Not going to shoot you. Just stand on that tile.'

Beck paused, but shrugged in a way that made it clear this was his choice. He went and stood on the tile.

Blake came over next to him. 'And look out – there, see? Past that ridge . . .'

Beck's eyes were growing accustomed to the dark. He could see the ridge; it loomed up, obscuring the stars.

'I was standing on precisely that spot when I saw your parents' plane explode. A ball of fire, lighting up the horizon . . . it was really quite beautiful. You should thank me.'

Beck turned and stared. '*Thank* you?'

'I *made* you, boy! Did you ever stop and think of that? Would you have lived the life you have if you still had Mummy and Daddy to go home to every day? You're like me in so many ways.'

'I am *so totally* unlike you!' Beck snapped back.

'Bah.' Blake waved a hand. 'Come on. You seek out danger. And why? Because you have a death wish. Don't deny it! No one gets into as much trouble as you by accident. All that stuff you do for Green Force is just an excuse. A means to an end. Every day you're pushing the world to the limit, you're saying, *Here I am, come and get me, do your worst!* And one day – yes, one day you know your luck will run out and the world will win. But what a life you'll have lived!'

'You are' – Beck couldn't find enough words in him to express what he felt – 'insane.'

'I'll prove it. Think back over the last fourteen years. All the things you've accomplished. Any regrets? I really don't think so. If you had a time machine, right now, tell me one thing, just one thing you'd go back and do differently.'

Beck looked him in the eye. 'I'd go back and I'd save Abby's life.'

And he meant it. It was what he'd been trying to

do right up until the last seconds before the explosion that killed her. It hadn't been his fault he'd been dragged away into the helicopter.

He had obviously spoiled Blake's little speech. He was supposed to admit that he had no regrets, proving that Blake had done him a favour by killing his parents.

James bit back a gasp.

Blake shot a scornful look in Beck's direction. 'Oh, please. You expect me to believe you'd be weak when you could be strong?'

His eyes narrowed and abruptly the gun was back in his hand. He drew back the hammer, aimed up into the night and fired. The *crack* of the bullet echoed around the mountains. The flash left a slowly-fading scar at the back of Beck's eyes.

And then Blake was offering it to him, handle first. 'Here. Take it. Go on!'

Beck took it, slowly.

'I've just proved it's loaded and the safety is off. You like to think you're so much better than me – that you stand for everything I'm against. Here's your chance to do something about it. You must realize, whether I take you down to the cellars and shoot you there, or just lock you up, your days of opposing me are over. You will never be free again, while I . . . I will just go on doing what I've done for the last seventy years, and when I'm gone, James will take over and carry on the work. You can change that now by shooting me. Go on! Stand by your convictions. End it. You can even shoot the boy too. In my desk, in the other room, are all the codes you will ever need to access Lumos's central mainframes – all our files, all our information. You'll have our resources and our wealth at your fingertips. You could take over! Just one twitch on that trigger. Go on!'

There was a certain logic to it. Of course, Beck knew he would never leave the monastery alive. But Blake was right. Without him at the helm, Lumos would be finished.

But what he would never understand was that Beck didn't want to rule the world and destroy people's lives. He just wanted to live in harmony with it. Lumos only understood control. It could never understand how you can be strong by being weak.

And so Beck put the safety catch back on and

chucked the pistol over the balustrade into the night. After a couple of seconds there was the *chink* of metal hitting rock.

A puff of breath and a gasp showed that James had stopped breathing during the last thirty seconds. His grandfather stepped back and surveyed the pair of them. Then he pressed a button on a device strapped to his wrist. A moment later, two guards appeared.

'My grandson needs a shower and a change of clothes. Sort it out. And this one' – he waved scornfully at Beck – 'to the cellar.'

Chapter 40

A shove in the small of his back sent Beck flying into the room. He just had time to make out the back wall and the outlines of wooden crates before the door slammed shut behind him and he was left in the dark. He heard the lock go.

He puffed his cheeks out. Still alive. That was a plus.

He had tried to keep track of the route as they brought him down here. Narrow passageways, steep stone steps. At the bottom was a vaulted stone room, lined with heavy wooden doors and dimly lit by a single bulb. He had just had time to make out barrels and boxes and other bits of junk. Then they had pushed him through one of the doors.

Beck stood in the darkness and slowly let the

room come to life around him. It wasn't pitch black. There was a band of light beneath the door. Shapes emerged from the gloom. The ceiling was very low – he could reach up a hand and touch it. His fingers brushed against rough plaster and cobwebs. He made his way slowly back to the door and felt the wall all around it, on either side. There did not seem to be a light switch. He explored the walls further until he had gone all round the room. The same dusty, rough plaster, but no switches. No doors or hatches either. No way out.

And, he couldn't help noticing, no heating. The cellar was basically the same temperature as the rock it was built into, and the rock was the same temperaure as the outside. It was not going to be a pleasant night. Beck was at least grateful they hadn't taken his clothes off him. He was still dressed for outdoors.

Something else that was definitely missing was food and water. How long were they going to keep him here? He shuddered, because it was quite possible that Edwin Blake did not intend to let him out. At all. Beck knew precisely how long the human body could go without food and water. He had spent a large part of his life finding both of them in strange places. Without food, he could still be alive a week from now or longer. Anyway, there would be spiders here, probably edible. He gave a strangled, snorting sort of laugh as he remembered something else: he also had his very own supply of maggots. It couldn't get much worse than that, Beck mused: eating maggots that had been feeding off your own body.

Of course, without water he would be dead in a couple of days. Slowly and painfully. And that was all there was to it. None of the tricks he knew about finding water would work here, because he was in a cellar buried deep in a mountain.

Well, deep in a monastery. The complex was so high up that even the deepest part of the basement was well above ground level. For all the good that did him.

But what was in the crates? he wondered. He could pick out the outlines of the jumbled pile against one wall. He made his way over and felt them with his hands. He winced as a splinter dug into his palm. They were just wooden packing crates, all empty. Nothing he could use for food. Nothing for warmth.

214

He turned one of them upside down so that he could sit on it, elbows on knees, chin in hands.

There was no point assuming that Blake would let him out again. The man had no need to. He had talked about shooting Beck in the cellar. Beck's one comfort was that he probably wouldn't do that. He would get much more of a buzz out of knowing that Beck was slowly starving to death.

And James? James could not be relied on. *Forget him*, Beck thought. James might or might not come good. Beck wasn't going to factor the other boy into his plans.

He got off the crate and lay down on the floor. He might as well try to sleep; it was pretty well the only useful thing he could do right now. He needed his strength for whatever lay ahead.

The stone floor was hard and uncomfortable, and the cold soaked into his bones. There was also a chill draught running across it. Beck got up again and stacked some of the crates together to make a bed. They were only slightly less uncomfortable, but he was out of the draught and off the floor that sucked the heat from his already cold limbs.

And then he was on his feet again, cursing himself for an idiot who didn't deserve to escape. If there was a draught, that meant air was moving. *From* somewhere, *to* somewhere. Which meant that the air had found another way out of this room.

He plucked a hair from his head and knelt down on the floor in front of the door, where the light was best. With his head almost touching the floor he held the hair between thumb and forefinger and watched it twitch in the breeze. The draught was blowing from under the door.

He shuffled on his knees a bit further into the room, and crouched down again to pick out the direction the hair was blowing in. Bit by bit, the hair led him over to one corner of the room. There was a narrow gap between the crates and the back wall. He pulled the crates away so that the light from the door could reach as much of the wall as possible, and bent close to the plaster to investigate.

There was no obvious grating or hole there. Beck licked his finger and held it up so that the draught tickled his wet digit. There, about halfway up the wall – that was where it was strongest.

He bent closer – and then he had it. A thin, hairline crack in the plaster. No doubt about it: air was going into it. Behind the plaster was a hollow space.

And then, out of nowhere, he remembered Sangmu talking about the history of the monastery. There had been a community living here before that, in a cave. In a network of caves. The monastery was built on top of it.

So where were the caves?

Presumably they were still here . . .

Beck picked up the nearest crate, held it above his head and smashed it down on the stone floor; then again, and once more after that. He wasn't worried about the noise. If there were any guards outside, he hoped they would think he was just smashing up the furniture out of frustration. The crate came apart, and now he had a tool – a length of wood with a jagged, pointed end.

He took a firm grip with both hands and jammed it into the crack.

Chapter 41

James came awake with a shudder and a gasp. It took him a moment to remember where he was. Soft mattress, duvet, moonlight shining faintly through the curtains . . .

Then he cursed and leaped out of bed. He hadn't meant to fall asleep! He should have just been lying there until everyone *thought* he was asleep. Big difference.

Granddad's instructions for a shower and a meal and a change of clothes had all been carried out. But then he had insisted on giving James the grand tour of the monastery. They had started at the top of the highest building and worked their way down to the lowest level. Almost the lowest level. James still remembered the archway and the flight of stone steps leading down. His granddad had just waved a dismissive hand.

'The cellars. Let's not disturb our little friend, eh?'

By the end of it all, James had felt like he had hung lead weights on his eyelids. Eventually the old man let him collapse into bed in one of the spare rooms.

And what time was it now? He fumbled for his watch and flicked the display on. Three o'clock. He winced. Could be worse. He could have slept till morning. Then he would have had to wait another day. He couldn't do this with anyone else around.

He swung his legs out of bed and quickly pulled on his clothes, then his boots and cagoule, stuffing his hat into his pocket. He intended to make a quick getaway. There wouldn't be time to come back to his room and get dressed for outdoors.

Then he quietly let himself out and made his way down to the lounge.

The monastery was quiet and its passage-ways were dim. James only froze at one point, hearing men's voices. Then he realized that he was passing by the communications room. Wherever he went, Granddad had staff manning the consoles twenty-four hours a day, bringing in information and helping him run his empire. But they were safely out of the way of where James was going.

Five minutes later he was in the lounge, peering into the little shrine set up for his mother. His eyes lingered on the smiling photograph. When had she last smiled like that? When had she last smiled like that *at him*? A long, long time ago. . .

James growled under his breath and reached for the door. And stopped. Supposing it was alarmed? What if he opened it up and the whole monastery went to red alert?

But then, why should it be alarmed? Who was Granddad expecting to come and steal anything?

He opened the case with a decisive tug and his fingers closed around the hard drive. 'Tah-dah!' he murmured. He slipped it into his pocket, closed the doors gently, and hurried quickly out of the room.

Chapter 42

The way down to the cellars was clear in his mind. *Thanks for showing me, Granddad.* But the stone steps weren't carpeted and the sound of his boots echoed in the narrow passageway.

James winced and gritted his teeth and forced himself to walk slowly.

In the vault at the bottom he could make out the outlines of the junk stored down there, but the corners were in shadow. There were several thick wooden doors set into the walls, but only one was closed. He went slowly up to it. There was a key in the lock, twisted so that it couldn't fall out.

He knocked gently. 'Beck?'

No reply. Well, what was he expecting? Beck had no reason to trust him. James looked forward to seeing the expression on his friend's face when he showed him the hard drive.

He turned the key and slowly pushed the door open. 'Beck?'

He almost stepped in, then paused. Supposing Beck was planning an escape? He could be hiding behind the door, ready to clobber the next guy who came in.

'It's me. James. I've got the hard drive . . .'

He pushed the door all the way open and saw Beck perched innocently on a wooden crate by the far wall. Almost too innocently. There were other crates stacked up behind him so that the wall itself was hidden from view.

James grinned. 'See?' He produced the hard drive. 'Look, I'm really sorry for all that – I mean, I know how you must feel, but I wasn't going to shoot you, honest! I was just bluffing. And I know I kicked you – I'm really sorry, but I had to or he wouldn't have believed me.'

Beck's expression froze halfway to a smile, then slowly crumpled. He buried his face in his hands and his voice was muffled. 'Oh . . . you . . . prat.'

'Huh?' James frowned. Beck wasn't being very grateful. 'What do you—?'

'Do you know your biggest mistake, James?' said his granddad behind him.

James gave a cry of surprise and leaped into the room.

His grandfather emerged from the shadows at the bottom of the steps, backed up by one of his bodyguards.

'Your biggest mistake,' he said conversationally, 'was that you never really provided a good reason for turning up here in the first place. OK, you said that Ian was bringing you – but why would he do that? And don't give me that rubbish about wanting to see Beck die – I thought he was already dead, remember, and Ian would not have wanted to admit he'd made a mistake! If he *had* discovered he was wrong, he would have quietly had Beck disposed of and no one would ever have known. So Ian was up to something, coming here, and you carried on with whatever it was. And now I know. My own grandson, my flesh and blood, a traitor.' His voice had slowly been growing colder; now it was arctic. 'I'll deal with you after a few days without food or water. That should put you in a receptive frame of mind.'

He reached in and pulled the door to, sealing James in with Beck and the darkness.

Chapter 43

'You get used to the dark,' Beck said. 'You'll be able to see in a moment.'

'Just in case it's not obvious,' James said bitterly, 'I came here to rescue you.'

'Yeah. How's that going?'

'I've had to make some adjustments to the plan.' James paused. 'Good news is, I've still got the drive . . .' He fished it out and gave it to Beck. 'Don't suppose he left a computer down here, did he?'

Beck looked down at the little object that had cost him so much. His eyes had got used to the gloom again. What he could see of James's face was a picture of misery. 'When you've finished feeling sorry for yourself, come and give me a hand?' he suggested.

James didn't move. 'I suppose the great Beck Granger has been able to dig a tunnel through solid rock . . .'

'Yeah, something like that.' Beck disappeared behind the small wall of packing cases that he had built. He had done it precisely so that no one who came in would see his handiwork. After a moment, out of curiosity, James came over to join him. He whistled when he saw the hole that Beck had opened up.

It was still only the size of a football, but it was much bigger than the hairline crack Beck had found.

'What's behind it?' James asked.

'A big empty space. I'm hoping it's the cave system they built this place on top of. The plaster is rock-solid – it takes ages to get through. I've been working on this for hours. But now there's two of us . . .'

James grabbed a piece of smashed-up wooden crate and went to work.

It took another hour to make a hole big enough for

them to squeeze through, one at a time, headfirst. Beck took the lead. His eyes strained in a darkness so deep it felt like something you could reach out and touch. Beneath his hands he felt cold, rough rock. He put a hand above his head and found that he was able to stand up straight without banging into a rocky ceiling.

'OK.' He spoke quietly but his voice echoed, and so he lowered it even further. This might not be the only place where the monastery covered a cave entrance. He didn't want their voices bouncing around the system and alerting anyone. 'Come on through.'

A few moments later, James joined him. He turned on his watch and let its minuscule light pick out their surroundings.

Beck had a brief impression of rocky walls and a tunnel stretching away into darkness. The draught was much stronger now – he could feel it moving against his skin. The sound echoed back up the cave, like some faraway machinery.

'Which way?' James whispered.

'Any way but back. Hold on.'

Beck reached back through the hole for the wooden plank he had been using as a tool. He tapped it against the floor, like a blind man might use a stick. If the floor suddenly fell away in front of them, or if they were about to walk into a dead end, then he would have some warning.

'We'll put out our left hands and stay in touch with the wall,' he murmured. 'If we ever come to a corner, we turn left.' And it sounded like there would be a lot of corners. Sangmu had said that the caves formed part of a whole network. But this way they would always be able to find their way back if they came to a dead end. 'Coming?'

The light from the hole soon fell away behind them. They were in the pitchest black Beck had ever known. The darkness was wrapped around them like velvet. It made no difference whether he opened or closed his eyes. Sparks of light and strange patterns from his retinas floated in front of his eyes, but he knew they were inside his head and nothing to rely on.

He still kept his eyes open. The tiniest glimmer of light will stand out in pitch black. If they ever came to any kind of opening to the outside, he wanted to see it. He didn't want to walk past and go further into the mountain.

Their only choice was to keep walking, and turning left, and hoping.

Sometimes they stumbled. A foot might catch a fallen rock or a hidden dip that the guide plank had missed.

Sometimes Beck felt the ceiling begin to brush his hair, and he had to call out a warning to the taller James and quickly duck down before he bashed his head.

Most of the time they could walk upright, twisting and turning with the cave.

When they finally saw the light, Beck at first thought it was just another random shape produced by his retinas. It was a slightly whiter splash of darkness. It could have been a few metres or a few kilometres away. But the breeze was suddenly stronger and the cave was growing smaller. The walls and the roof closed in until the boys could only walk at a crouch, but by now they could clearly see the way out.

An iron grating blocked their way, but it wasn't cemented in and the rock around it had crumbled. Their combined strength was enough to shift it and make it break free. They crawled out into the open air. Finally.

They still had the precious hard drive. They had made it. So far.

Chapter 44

They emerged on the ridge behind a bush, halfway between the top of the stone steps and the monastery. Beck stood up slowly and flexed his back. The tops of the mountains to the east were tipped with orange flame. Dawn was coming. Light was spilling over the valley and Blake's private airfield. He crouched down behind the bush again.

James took a deep breath of outside air. 'Oh, man, that feels good! We're free!'

'We're still inside the fence,' Beck pointed out.

'We're . . . almost free. Think we can make it back to Sangmu's?'

Beck peered out across the valley. It was clear of bushes and trees. There was nowhere for two boys to hide. 'Not like this. And even if we could – we shouldn't. The moment they find us missing, they'll scour the village. They'll be able to move a lot faster than we can and there's more of them. No – we need another plan.'

'Like what?'

Beck simply pointed at the airstrip – and the two aeroplanes at the end of it.

James whistled. 'You think big. Can you fly one of those?'

'I had a lesson. Once. I could maybe manage the small one. The one with the propeller.'

'Shame,' James mused. 'It would be kinda neat to steal Granddad's private jet . . . OK, so now we just have to reach the plane without being seen.' He frowned. 'That's still going to be hard. Very hard.'

From the foot of the steps, the track led across the valley. It veered round the airstrip and carried on to the gate in the fence. Beck narrowed his eyes in thought. The two planes, and their little hangar, were also at the end of the airstrip. In theory, they could head towards the planes and always keep the hangar between them and the guards on the gate. But it would be risky, and they would be perfectly visible to anyone looking out of the monastery.

And then, as his eyes fixed on a speck in the distance, Beck laughed. Suddenly there was a plan in his mind, clear as day.

'I think we can do that. Look who's coming. Remember she said she was doing today's supply run?'

James peered out, and his face broke into a grin. 'Sangmu!'

A human figure and a mule were plodding down the track from the far side of the valley, towards the gate. The mule was loaded up with panniers – big, deep baskets strapped to either side.

'While everyone's looking her way – come on.'

Beck quickly jumped to his feet, and James had to follow suit. They trotted down the steps as quickly as they could. For about half a minute, anyone in the monastery could have looked down and seen them. Beck felt his back growing hot, as if laser sights were burning into it.

But there were no shouts, no alarms ringing out into the clear mountain air. They reached the storehouse and pressed themselves against the wooden wall.

'Found the door,' James said. 'It's not locked.'

'Why would it be? The fence is meant to keep people out. Quick, get in.'

The inside was lined with shelves and boxes. They lurked behind the door until, ten minutes later, they heard the sound of hooves coming to a halt outside. The door opened and a figure shuffled in. It was wrapped in padded mountain clothing and laden with boxes. Despite his assurance, Beck had to hope that Sangmu hadn't suddenly gone and swapped with someone else. It was a chance he had to take.

'Give you a hand with that?' he asked softly.

The figure jumped and exclaimed, 'Beck!' She put the boxes down on the floor and hugged him. 'When you didn't come back last night . . . What happened?'

Beck and James exchanged glances.

'Long story,' Beck said.

'Very long,' James agreed.

'Did you get what you wanted?'

Beck patted the pocket containing the hard drive. 'Oh yes. Now we just need to get as far as the aeroplanes. And I think I know how we can do it.'

Briefly, Beck outlined the plan that had come to him when he had seen her approaching.

Sangmu looked thoughtful. She stepped back and surveyed each of them in turn, running her eyes from their heads to their feet, and nodded.

'Yes. Yes, I think we can do that, though it will not be comfortable . . .'

Chapter 45

Sangmu was right, Beck thought. It was not comfortable.

He was curled up so tightly that every joint was on fire. His knees pressed into his chest and compressed his lungs. His injured leg was agony and he couldn't do anything to shift himself and relieve the pressure.

The panniers strapped to the mule were exactly the right size to hold a fourteen-year-old boy, bent double. They could get from the monastery to the planes in broad daylight. Anyone who looked in their direction would see exactly what they expected to see – a mule with panniers strapped on either side, and Sangmu walking next to it. Beck could see the approaching hangar through gaps in the pannier's wicker sides.

His vision lurched with every step the mule took.

But *boy*, was it uncomfortable. Beck found two sources of consolation: the tall, gangly James was probably suffering even more, and they were nearing the planes.

Finally they were so close to the end of the airstrip that the hangar was the only thing he could see. They were out of sight of the guards at the gate. The mule stopped plodding.

'We're as close as we can get,' Sangmu whispered. 'Get out now.'

Beck and James erupted from their panniers like a pair of jack-in-the-boxes. They both climbed down to the ground, grunting and stretching.

Sangmu was immediately walking again. 'I can't wait. They will notice if there's a delay.'

'I know,' Beck whispered back. 'Thanks. We'll come and see you.'

'Thank you for helping me to keep my promise to your mother, Beck. Good luck.'

Beck smiled as Sangmu led the mule away and disappeared behind the hangar. Beck and James headed in the other direction.

The plane Beck intended to take sat facing the executive jet on a tarmac apron in front of the hangar. It looked similar to the one he'd had his one flying lesson in. The passenger sat behind the pilot and the cockpit canopy slid shut over them.

They crept forward, bending low, to pull the chocks out from in front of the wheels. Then they climbed up onto the wings and peered into the cockpit. The controls were duplicated in the rear section so that the plane could be flown from the front or the back. And there were a lot of controls. Beck forced himself to remember that this was all relatively simple. He didn't need *all* the controls – just the ones that made the plane fly . . .

The canopy was shut, but there was a handle marked RELEASE and the canopy slid backwards when Beck pulled on it. He was pleased to see that there were parachutes already set into the seats. They could just climb in and put on the straps at the same time as they fastened their seat belts. A headset with a pair of earphones and a mike hung next to the control stick. Beck put his on and told James to do the same. Once the engine had fired up they wouldn't be able to hear each other normally.

Beck flicked the switch marked INTERCOM, and after a moment James's voice crackled in his ears.

'OK, so, you have done this before, right?'

'Oh, yeah,' Beck said casually. His eyes scanned the other switches and dials in front of him. 'The instructor let me take off and everything.' Which wasn't quite true. He had been allowed to keep his hands and feet on the duplicate controls while the instructor did the actual flying – but he didn't want to tell James that at this point.

He had it! A switch marked START. Sounded simple enough. Beck got ready to press it in with his thumb. After this, there would be no turning back. Once that engine started, every guard would be roused.

He pushed the button firmly.

Chapter 46

'All OK?' James sounded doubtful. Beck barely heard him. Nothing was happening!

Then, just as he was about to take his thumb away, the engine coughed. A cloud of smoke blew out of the exhausts. With a rising whine that turned into a roar, the propeller began to spin.

James had only now spotted the missing link in Beck's flying lessons. 'Hang on . . .'. Did he let you land as well?'

'Uh – no.'

'Uh – isn't that kind of important . . . ?'

The plane wasn't moving. Beck found the lever marked BRAKES and let it go. The plane twitched, but that was all. The throttle! It was pulled right back, so the engine was on minimum revs. He wrapped his fingers around it and pushed it slowly forward. The engine roared twice as loud. The plane shuddered, and began to move.

Heading straight for the jet.

James shrieked in Beck's ears as Beck kicked down hard on the rudder pedal. The plane swerved round, violently enough to tilt up on one of its wheels. Beck kicked on the other pedal to straighten up and pulled back on the throttle to slow down again.

Now they were facing down the runway. This was it. Beck glanced over to one side. They were in view of the guards now, and the men were all looking their way. Maybe they didn't know who was in the plane, but they could surely tell that it wasn't an expert at the controls. It was time to go.

The plane started to trundle forward in a straight line. Beck pushed the throttle hard forward. The engine roared again and the plane began to speed up.

But it was still only trundling along at a fast walking pace. Beck knew it was nowhere near take-off speed, even though the whole frame shook with the power of the engine. He ran his mind back to that one lesson. What was it? *Think, think* . . .

'Um, they're coming . . .' James shouted.

Some of the men had left the guard post and were running purposefully towards them.

Beck's eyes fell on a lever marked PITCH. Of course! Pitch controlled the angle of the propeller blades as they cut through the air. And that changed the amount of thrust you got out of them. For driving around on the ground you only wanted a little thrust, just enough to keep the plane moving. For taking off, you wanted lots and lots.

Beck moved the lever to its fullest setting. The plane roared and the acceleration pushed him back into his seat. James whooped in his ears as the plane hurled itself forward.

Now, how fast did this thing have to be going to take off? There was a notch on the speed dial at the sixty mark. Beck hoped and trusted that this was the one. The needle seemed to crawl up towards it.

The tail wheel had left the ground and the plane was running horizontally on its two wing wheels. The needle reached sixty and Beck pulled back on the stick.

The ground fell away. They were airborne.

'Yeah, baby!' James shouted happily. And then: 'Uh, Beck. I think they're, uh, shooting at us . . .'

Beck's head whipped round. Far below, the guards were kneeling down, their guns raised to their shoulders. All he could see was little flashes of light flickering at the end of the barrels.

Suddenly a line of small holes appeared in the left wing tip, like it had just been run over by a giant sewing machine. The plane lurched to the right. Beck instinctively flinched and pushed the stick over the other way. The plane swerved like it was falling out of the sky. Beck's stomach seemed to have been left behind somewhere. He pulled the stick back again to straighten out.

'They can't shoot me! I'm their boss's grandson!' James yelped.

'They don't know that,' Beck muttered. 'They just know the plane's been stolen . . .'

The throttle was still at full power. They should be going as fast as they could but the plane was shuddering like a car in the wrong gear. He remembered that changing pitch again, once they were up, would help the airspeed. He pushed the pitch lever halfway back to its old position. The shuddering died down and he felt the plane pick up speed once more.

But the guards were still shooting. And then, suddenly, there was a clattering in front of him as if someone was smashing up a load of machinery. The engine belched and shuddered and a cloud of black smoke suddenly blew back over the cockpit.

They had been hit. The engine was losing power and the plane began to fall out of the sky.

Chapter 47

Beck ignored James's yells. All his attention was on coordinating the throttle and the pitch lever and the control stick and the rudder pedals. The plane was still falling, but somehow he found a magic combination that made the engine cough back into life.

It only had a fraction of its old power, but they were high enough that they could afford to descend a little. They had left the high valley of the monastery, and were now out of shooting range.

Beck looked out at the peaks that soared around them. 'I'm going to try and go round that mountain ahead,' he shouted. 'If we put it between them and us, it'll buy us some time.'

'Right,' came the nervous response. 'In the unlikely event that we survive . . .'

Heart pounding, Beck pulled back on the stick. The nose of the plane tilted up but the engine sound grew even more laboured. He felt his ears pop and glanced at the altimeter. They were pointing upwards, but they were falling.

He pushed the throttle forward to feed more power to the engine. It continued to cough and splutter, but the propeller seemed more effective now. The altimeter showed that they were going up again, little by little.

Unfortunately, the fuel gauge was visibly dropping. The guards must have holed the tank. Beck was just glad that the whole plane hadn't blown up on the spot.

'Uh, Beck?' said the voice in his ears. 'We seem to be going up. Don't we want to go down?'

'Oh, we'll go down,' Beck said confidently. That was the one part he could absolutely guarantee. The plane was shaking all around him. The fuel needle had dropped down into the red; smoke was still billowing out of the engine casing.

The mountain loomed ahead, and he nudged on the stick to take them round it. The ground dropped away even further on the other side; below them he saw thick cloud. The sides of a deep valley rose out of it, laced with snow. There was lots more space for the plane, and them, to fall out of. *Yes!* Beck thought.

'Oh, blimey!' James had seen the same thing. 'It's miles down! You've got to take us down now!'

'I'm not taking us down. We're jumping.'

'*Eh?*'

Beck made himself sound calm, though his heart was thumping in his chest. 'I don't know how to land – we're going to crash anyway – and if we don't, then the plane will probably just blow up first. We need to get out. It's easy. We've got parachutes.'

'I hate you, Beck Granger!' James shrieked.

'Consider it payback for kicking me!'

The engine was spluttering, at its last gasp. Beck issued the instructions quickly and urgently: 'There's a handle on your parachute harness – on the left, by your waist.'

'Got it.'

'The moment you're out of the plane, pull on it. Once your chute opens, there'll be handles on straps by your shoulders. Pull on them to go left or right.

You'll have plenty of time to practise. When you come in to land, pull on both of them together. That'll slow you down and you'll touch down gently. Hopefully.' Beck paused. 'Now, open the canopy 'cos I can't take my hands off the controls.'

Another pause, and then the canopy slid back. Freezing wind laced with oily smoke blasted into the cockpit.

'Undo your seat belt,' Beck shouted. He fumbled with his buckle to release his own.

'Done. Do I climb out now?'

'No need.' Beck pushed the stick hard over to one side. The plane flipped over onto its back and they both simply dropped out like bombs into the clear air.

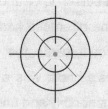

Chapter 48

Beck's body fell, totally out of control, through the whiteout of the clouds. Hurricane-force winds pummelled him from every side. This wasn't the careful, planned skydiving he had done before. It wasn't even like the time he'd had to bail out of a smugglers' plane flying over the Sahara. He felt like a doll in a freezing tumble drier. And he wasn't wearing goggles, so his eyes immediately teared up in the airflow and he couldn't see a thing.

Beck scrabbled at the handle on his harness and tugged. With a sound like the sky splitting open, his chute was ripped out of its pack.

He swung like a pendulum beneath the canopy, round and round. Out in the clouds, everything was still white. He was still half-blinded by tears, but finally he felt his insides settling down and opened his eyes. Far below, a plume of smoke had to be the plane, still heading down towards the ground. Through the clouds, James's chute was a splash of colour, apparently falling smoothly and under control. *Great!* Beck decided he would steer over towards his friend so that they could stay close together. But first he would have to lose some height.

The way to do that was to spin down in a tight spiral, which made you drop more quickly. He tugged on one of the handles by his shoulder and felt his chute tip over to the right. He came round in a full half-circle – and cried out in surprise.

He hadn't realized that he was close to the side of the mountain. It had been lurking behind him, and now there it was, right in front. A massive wall of rock – and he was heading straight for it. He pulled hard on the strap again and began to turn. He had to get away from it, right away.

A ledge loomed below him, and suddenly he knew he wasn't going to make it. He just had time to grit his teeth and pull on the straps to cut his speed, and—

BANG! He crashed into the rock. There was a wrench and a crack in his arm, and a spear of agony ran up from elbow to shoulder. Rough rock scraped against his face, and then he was falling again. His chute had collapsed and spilled out all its precious air. He was a jumbled mass of boy and silk, tumbling down the side of a rocky slope.

Abruptly he was yanked to a standstill. The chute had caught on something. The ropes twanged around him. His arm took the opportunity to send a red-hot jab into him, and he clenched his teeth against a scream. *Ahh, that hurt!*

But finally he was still, dangling in a tangled web over a very vertical precipice.

So he could finally do something about his situation. Maybe he could pull himself up . . .

He tried to reach the straps. Only one arm moved. The other hung uselessly at his side. He glared at it and tried to force it into action. Nothing happened. He was pretty sure his shoulder was broken.

No, he couldn't pull himself up. Not single-handed. Not like this.

He gazed down. Beyond his feet was only the top

of clouds. He had no way of knowing how high up he was.

Beck closed his eyes.

He had looked death in the eye many times – considerably more than most fourteen-year-olds. But even in the darkest times, there had always been a way out.

He couldn't see one now.

If he stayed here, dangling, death was one hundred per cent certain. If he dropped . . .

Ninety nine per cent? It all depended on how close the ground was, on the other side of those clouds. And there was only one way to find out. Beck knew he had no choice. Stay and die alone, or drop and risk it. He didn't want to wait any longer. It would just give him more time to freak out and do nothing. He knew he had to act.

With his good hand Beck felt for the release buckle of his chute. It was difficult to hold it and twist it like you were meant to. It was designed for two hands.

And one day . . .

An old man's voice seemed to whisper in his ears, bitter and full of hate.

252

. . . yes, one day, you know your luck will run out and the world will win. But what a life you'll have lived until that day!

The buckle opened up with a loud *snap!* and he tumbled into the clouds.

Chapter 49

Beck blinked in confusion. Somehow he knew he wasn't really here. He should be falling, twisting in mid-air, hurtling towards the solid ground. He wasn't ten years younger, sitting on his mother's lap with her arms around him while they watched a video play out on a laptop.

He struggled to turn round and look at her, but her arms held him tight. Her voice spoke in his ear. He could feel her breath tickle the side of his face.

'Watch, sweetheart. Watch and learn.'

On the screen, a mother snow leopard sat calm and impassive while three little cubs gambolled around her.

'They really are like cats,' his mother's voice said. 'They hunt what they can and eat what they can. They prefer small animals – their size or less. They generally steer clear of humans, if they can.'

Another leopard lurked in the bushes, a larger male, eyes were fixed firmly on the cubs. It tensed, ready to pounce, and suddenly the mother leopard was there on top of it. The sleek, muscular bodies of the two adults wrapped around each other in a furious whirlwind of teeth and claws. The mother opened up a bloody gash across the male's snout. He turned and fled.

'They'll defend their children with their lives. With everything they've got.'

And then the scene onscreen changed again. One of the cubs had climbed a tree and had no idea how to get down again. It was giving out unhappy little squeaks. The mother jumped up and grabbed it in her mouth by the scruff of its neck. Then she carefully backed down the way she had come and dropped the cub gently back onto the ground.

'So you see, a mother will do anything for her cubs. Fight for them, defend them, help them. See how she's carrying her baby? He knows his mum's looking out for him, and that makes him the safest baby in the world.'

Beck marvelled that being held in a leopard's mouth counted as 'safe'.

Suddenly the arms tightened in a farewell hug.

'Oh, darling, I think you've seen enough. You can go now.'

Little Beck began to cry. He didn't want to go . . .

Chapter 50

Beck opened sore eyes and immediately squeezed them shut again. The cloud had gone and the sky was a blue canopy above him. He lay and basked in the sun's heat.

At the back of his mind he knew that every part of his body hurt as though he had been beaten with a baseball bat. A safety fuse in his brain was stopping him from feeling all the pain, all at once. He wiggled his toes and fingers experimentally. They moved. The rest of him . . . The rest of him felt like it could move, if it had to. But he would really rather it didn't.

There was something important going on. He frowned as he tried to remember what it was. He had a dim memory of being suspended in space, air rushing past him. Then a massive blow that shocked the consciousness out of him.

There was something cold and wet at his finger-tips. In fact, he was lying in it. Like the pain, the cold and wet were only an issue if you thought about them. It was much easier to lie here and feel warm and woozy.

Warm and woozy.. . . That rang a bell, and he didn't like it. In fact, he felt annoyed that two such nice, snug words had such a bad sound to them. What was wrong with *warm and woozy*? He had been told about people who felt that way. It was the kind of thing you felt if . . . hang on . . . if you were . . .

Oh yeah. Dying.

Nope, not dying today, he resolved. With a huge mental effort, he summoned his mind back into his body. It came crashing down – along with all the pain and cold he had been trying not to feel, and a terrible, parching thirst. He opened his eyes again, cautiously.

A vertical wall of rock rose above him. The cloud had gone and he could see all the way up to the sky. If he squinted, he could make out a patch of colour high above. The parachute, still snagged. He was lying on his back in snow. It was a brilliant, pure white that gleamed in the sun. He could only allow himself a quick glimpse before he felt the world start to spin and he had to close them again. How could just lying down and looking up make him dizzy?

'Cos you've got concussion, brainiac, he told himself. *Look how far you fell!*

He sneaked another look up at the cliff. Oh yeah. Quite a way.

Beck tried to lift his head and look around. It made the world spin again and he had to let it fall back, but he just had time to spot something dark lying a short distance away. He kept his head pointing in that direction so he didn't have to exert himself. He frowned. It was a tyre. A tyre, half buried in snow, halfway up a mountain. How did that get there?

But in fact there was more to it than that. The tyre was still attached to the wheel. The wheel was attached to a metal strut . . .

It was an aircraft wheel. He must have come down where the plane had crashed.

No, he couldn't have. He and James had fallen

straight down. The plane had kept going. This must be another plane.

Beck's heart began to pound as he realized which other plane it might be. And then he froze, and stopped thinking about planes. Because right opposite him, about twenty metres away, was a snow leopard, quietly sitting on a rock. It was watching him through unblinking eyes.

He remembered the snarling blur of teeth and claws that had attacked that bull. This was not a creature that showed mercy. The rush of blood made Beck feel woozy again.

They really are like cats, his mother had said . . .

Beck frowned. 'Huh?'

He remembered the conversation. He couldn't recall when he'd had it. It was like seeing something that suddenly reminded you of a dream you had completely forgotten. It was fresh in his mind – but it couldn't be, because his mum had died ten years ago.

They hunt what they can and eat what they can. They prefer small animals, their size or less.

His mum's interest in leopards had taught him that cute does not equal safe. Beck knew all too well the danger he was in right now. But he couldn't even stand up without feeling dizzy.

His mum had said that snow leopards tried to steer clear of humans. It suddenly became very important to make this creature realize that he was a human, not just conveniently injured prey.

'My mum told me a lot about you,' he told it. Would a human voice do the trick? 'She was nice. You'd have liked her.'

Then another memory came to him. Sangmu had said that a family of snow leopards had taken over the crash site.

'Maybe you met her . . .'

And then Beck was struck by a sudden spark of hope. Sangmu and her people had been to the crash site. Which meant that there was a way up.

Or, from his point of view, a way down.

'Right, my snow leopard friend,' he said. 'It's been lovely, but I've got to go . . .'

He counted under his breath – one, two, three – and heaved himself upright. '*Aargh!*'

He collapsed face down in the snow. His broken arm had given way under him . . .

Chapter 51

'This,' Beck mumbled into the snow, 'is going to take a while.'

He struggled to his knees. With his good hand, he clamped his broken arm to his side. The snow leopard had jumped down from its rock and was pacing a couple of metres away.

'Oh, give me a break. Don't start eating me until I'm really dead. Deal?'

The animal gave a kind of snort and padded over to a snow bank. It scraped a small hole in the snow with claws that could have disembowelled him with a single blow. They snagged on a bright orange strap. The snow leopard worked its mouth into the hole and grabbed the strap between its jaws. It growled and backed away, tugging the whatever-it-was with it.

Then it let go, and looked at Beck with an expression that seemed to say, *Go on, then.*

And Beck watched in disbelief as it calmly strolled away. 'Huh?'

He shuffled over to the strap on his knees. It seemed to be made of fluorescent plastic. He gave it a pull, then reached out with his good hand and scraped more of the snow away. The outlines of a plastic case began to emerge. Handwritten in black magic marker, he could just make out the words MELANIE GRAN—

All at once he was digging with all the strength of his one good hand. The box came free with a final tug. It was the size of a food cooler bag, fastened with a pair of plastic catches. Parts of it had been badly scorched but the case was intact. The catches snapped up and Beck pulled the lid open.

Inside was a satellite phone, nestling in a specially shaped layer of foam.

'Oh, you're kidding,' he breathed. 'Not that there'll be any juice left after ten years . . .'

He took the phone out anyway. The foam

layer also came out. There was more equipment beneath it.

A mini satellite dish, which opened up like an umbrella. He could set it on a little tripod and point it south to where satellites orbited the Earth's equator.

A small black panel which opened up at the flick of a switch.

Of course, Beck thought. *Genius. A simple solar charger.* His mum and dad were smart! He could lay it on the snow and it gleamed like a mirror reflecting the sun.

And cables, to join everything together. He fumbled excitedly.

He sat with his back to the rock and the phone on his lap. The display glowed into life. The word CHARGING showed in one corner.

And, in another, SIGNAL LOCK.

'I don't believe it . . .'

What were the chances?

A mother will do anything for her cubs . . .

Suddenly he felt it. She was here. Somehow she had brought her cub to this place and provided this phone. He was as safe as that cub in its mother's mouth.

He looked up for the leopard. 'Um, thanks . . . ?'

It was nowhere to be seen.

'Thanks, Mum,' Beck whispered to the world at large.

Then, with a trembling finger, he touched the keypad. It lit up, waiting for input.

What time was it back in London? he wondered. Six-hour time difference. Very early hours of the morning.

Someone was about to get a disturbed night, but Beck expected he would be forgiven.

He began to dial the number he knew by heart. The number for home.

Chapter 52

BLAKE TAKEN

Al held the newspaper up for Beck to read the headline. It took up most of the front page. Beck glanced at it and smiled, but he already knew the story. He settled back into his comfortable, cushioned seat. Outside the plane, the taxiway slowly rolled past. They were almost at the end of the runway, ready to take off.

'It worked.' Al sounded immensely pleased with himself as he scanned the page. 'He stepped off a plane right into the hands of the US Marshals.'

Edwin Blake must have realized that, with the hard drive gone, his time was up. Later that day he had fled the monastery in his jet. He must have had half a dozen escape routes planned, just in case. He disappeared.

But if Blake had moved fast, Green Force moved faster. He hid. They went public. They published everything that was on the hard drive. Every single little note, every figure, every slide, every file went online. It was posted on a hundred different servers around the world so that Lumos could never get them all taken down.

All the corruption, pollution and deception. Rogue bank accounts, hidden environmental reports, lists of bribes – you name it. And one piece of evidence led to another. Lumos would be sunk – Al was certain of it.

And Lumos turned on its creator. Someone, somewhere in the organization knew where Blake was, and they gave him away. He thought he was entering the USA anonymously. In fact, he was arrested the moment his feet touched the ground.

The airliner's engines went to full throttle and the plane surged down the runway. Its nose tilted and the ground fell away. Beck settled back into his seat. After several months, he finally got to leave Nepal.

'How's the shoulder?' Al asked. He only asked it two or three times a day now.

Beck gave it an experimental wiggle. Then he rested his head against the seat-back and closed his eyes. It had been a long day. 'Still aches when it gets cold.'

'Good.' Al gave him a prod. 'It can remind you that you're mortal and maybe stop you from doing anything *incredibly and utterly stupid* ever again.'

Beck opened an eye. 'Are you ever going to forgive me?'

'Ask me when you're thirty. We'll see how it's going.'

Beck smiled and closed his eyes again.

At first Al hadn't believed that Beck was alive. When he heard Beck's voice on the phone, Al genuinely thought that he must have gone mad with grief. But once he accepted that it really was his nephew talking, he was on to the Green Force office in Kathmandu. Their helicopter had picked Beck up two hours later.

Soon after that they found James, alive and well.

Though, being James, he had managed to land in a river, and had almost been swept away to his death in a tangle of parachute cords, but had been pulled out at the last moment by some helpful Sherpas who had seen him drop from the sky. Good old James. The Sherpas had stripped him and wrapped him in yak blankets and sat him next to a warm fire and saved his life. He claimed it had been the most unpleasant experience he'd ever had.

'Those blankets were *scratchy*, and they were right against my skin . . .'

And then had come the months of wrangling.

Getting out of Nepal wasn't quite as easy as Beck had hoped. For a start the Nepalese authorities weren't very happy to learn that there was no record of his entering the country. They were even less impressed when they learned that he was officially dead. He could truthfully say that he had lost his passport, but the UK passport office preferred to issue new ones only with birth certificates, not death certificates too. So while Al had been able to come and go, Beck had had to kick his heels in the care of the local Green Force office in Kathmandu until all the paperwork was sorted out. That was until James – who had always been alive, and still had a passport – had swooped in and put him up in a decent hotel. Beck had spent the time relaxing and convalescing, exercising gently to get his injured shoulder and leg back to full strength. His leg had been treated with antibiotics – which was way less icky than maggots – and he would always have a deep scar. However, not many people would get to see it.

Beck, Al and James had been to see Sangmu and had retrieved Beck's mother's ashes. The simple box was in a case in the hold, flying home with them. And now, finally, they were leaving.

'You know another reason I didn't recognize you on the phone?' Al asked. 'Apart from being dead? Your voice has changed. You're getting older.'

'Really?' Beck replied. 'No wonder you're a professor!' He rested his head on his uncle's shoulder. Al wiggled his arm free and slid it round Beck's shoulders.

'How do you think you'll cope without Lumos to fight?' Al asked later as they ate their airline dinner together.

Beck paused. The idea had come to him as they were looking out of the window and saw the Himalayas' most famous peak. He had instantly recognized the grey-black hump of Everest. The peak was splashed with the last orange rays of the setting sun. *Of course*, Beck had thought. It was as if the plan had been staring down at him from the roof of the world all along.

'I've got a bigger adversary now,' he said lightly.

'Oh . . . ?' Al tried to keep it light, but Beck picked up the hint of worry. And warning.

He smiled. 'I'm going to climb Everest one day. And I'm going to scatter Mum's ashes from the top.'

Al peered out of the window and sighed. He was quiet for a moment; then he felt Beck's hand and turned to look into Beck's eyes. 'You just never, ever give up, do you, Beck?'

'I've been taught well,' Beck replied with a wry smile, and the pair started to laugh together.

'Yes, you have.'

The plane pointed its nose towards home and they flew west, into the sunset.

BEAR'S SURVIVAL TIPS

MAKING A FIRE

In *Lair of the Leopard*, Beck makes a campfire to keep them warm in the mountains. Fire can seem like your one true friend when you are in a wild and hostile environment. But it is a friend that must always be treated with respect and care.

With a match and something to burn, making a fire can be simple. Beck builds a pile of kindling – small, dry twigs – in a hollow in the ground.

Bigger sticks are laid on top like the frame of a tepee. Beck strikes a match and holds it to the kindling.

Once the fire has taken, he lays branches over the hollow to block out draughts, with a space for smoke to escape in the centre.

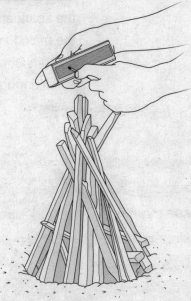

The basic elements of laying a fire are as follows:

LOCATION
Wind direction and how close the fire will be to your shelter are the most important factors.

TINDER
Without a match, you will need a flint and steel and some tinder, such as cotton material that can be ignited easily.

KINDLING

Kindling must burn long enough to take the spark and allow the main fuel source to catch alight. It must be small enough to ignite easily.

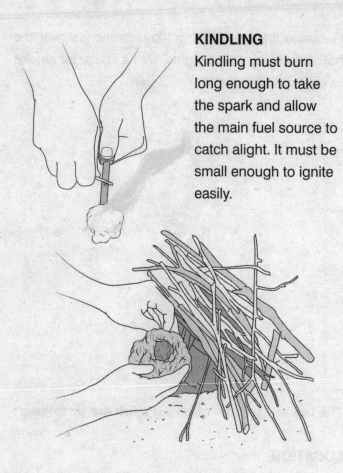

FUEL

This must keep the fire burning, ideally slowly and steadily. Softwoods burn intensely, and with more smoke and less heat than hardwoods. Hardwoods are harder to ignite but leave smouldering coals.